ISBN-10: 0985741724

ISBN-13: 978-0-9857417-2-3

Library of Congress Control Number: 2015935306
Pressea Publishing, Garden Grove, CA

Outlander Leander: Vol.3

The General's Bust

By:
Eisah

Edited by:
Laurie Laliberte of the Kindle All-Stars

Illustrations by:
Silvia Texidó Viyuela [Lylith]

Table of Contents

4, 27, 3399
Waddersday

She sat inside the police station, staring at the pile of letters. They were battered and crinkled. Dragging the top one off the pile, she held it in her coarse hands. While she waited for someone to come, she leafed through them, leaving the letters inside the envelopes. She didn't need to open them. Every word was etched in her mind.

While she stared at the envelope, she recited its contents in her head. Each one induced a flood of memories that drowned her in an endless whirlpool of words. When her gaze lifted, the station was bustling with life. Men and women rushed in every direction while the world around her remained still.

Footsteps caught her ears as a young man in uniform approached. Thick curls were tied loosely behind his back. His nose curved outward, while his ears curved towards the back of his head. His skin was a gorgeous russet, his hair several shades darker. A young man just beginning his life.

She pushed the letters into her satchel. He stopped in front of her and gave her a handsome smile. "Mrs. Breigah?" He knelt down on one knee.

Under different circumstances she may have hit on him. As much as she loved her husband, it had been six long years since he passed, and the tree grown from his remains was a horrible conversationalist, and an even worse lover. But her mind was too preoccupied today.

"Yes." She nodded. "Have you found anything?"

"I'm sorry, Ma'am. We haven't found any leads," he said, extending a hand to her. "I promise we'll contact you right away if we find anything."

"Are you certain?" She placed her hand in his. He stood, and gently pulled her up.

"Yes, I'm sure. Is there anything else I can help you with?" he asked as he escorted her towards the entrance. "A drink?"

"No." She shook her head. "No thank you."

He nodded. When they reached the door, he placed a hand on her shoulder, looked into her eyes, and reassured her, "We'll call."

She nodded once and he left her there. Her gaze wandered back into the police station. People were still busy. They had no time to pore over one case.

Cold air nipped her face when she pushed through the door. A few flecks of snow blew by. She wrapped herself in her heavy coat and looked down the unfamiliar streets.

No leads. No leads. *No leads*. There were never any leads. Leads wouldn't be handed to them. As well-intentioned as they might have been, no one cared like she did.

Holding her coat as the wind threatened to take it, she leaned on her cane and trudged down the street. She followed the dim glow of the street lights towards the sleepless parts of the city.

If they didn't have any leads, she would have to make one.

4, 27, 3399
Waddersday

"I was on my way here, walking down the street when I felt something light hit my head. At first I thought it was a leaf."

I sat across from Rykiel, listening as he intently told his story, his expression fluctuating with every sentence. He had the same puffy, short hair he'd had for decades and the same white and red uniform all the soldiers wore. Like many soldiers, he had a pink tassel hanging at his right hip.

"It rolled off and I glanced down. But when I looked, a wesp was clinging to my pant leg!" He laid an arm on the table. His eyes narrowed. "It was a terrible time to be deathly allergic to wesps."

I pictured the thin, black insect climbing up his pant leg. It had two red stripes down its back, translucent wings and large jaws.

"I tried to shake it off but it wouldn't go away. I looked straight into its eyes and let me tell you," he leaned forward, two fingers pointing at his eyes, "it had murderous intentions. So I held my pant leg away from my skin in case it tried to bite me."

I painted angry eyebrows on the insect in my mind.

"Someone had a hose filling up a pond in their front yard, so I sidled over to it," he moved in his chair as if he was shuffling to the side, "trying to keep my pant leg away from my skin. It was hanging over a tiny fence, so I managed to reach it without bending over. I yanked on it with one hand until I got to the end." He motioned with a make believe hose, pointing it at his white pant leg, then raised his voice, "Then I sprayed the bugger off me!" Rykiel leaned forward, holding up a hand and making a loose chopping motion with it as he reached the end of his story. "And *that's* why my pants are wet."

Should I give a standing ovation for that performance? "That's almost exciting as the story of how you nearly died at the dentist." I chuckled.

"That was a harrowing day." He collapsed into his chair, stabbing one of his meatballs with his fork and munching on it. I briefly wondered if his secret to keeping his youthful looks was acting like a kid. Rykiel was in his forties, but he looked like he was thirty, maybe younger. The only wrinkles on his face were laugh lines.

I knew Dad had asked him to check in on me but, truth be told, I was secretly grateful. When I was younger, Rykiel was a daily staple in my life. Then, when I was about eight, he had his first daughter. Understandably, I wasn't his first priority after that. Once I became a teenager, I barely saw him anymore. Dad didn't need anyone to babysit me, and I didn't have to go with my dad on trips to the base.

Now Rykiel would take me out for food, or stop by my house about twice a month. I was glad to see him again, even if it meant hiding my career choice from another person.

I set my utensils down on my empty plate. Rykiel insisted on paying, like he always did. People from my dad's generation were always stubborn about taking anything from the younger ones.

Still, I wanted to do something for him, too.

"I know some people at the theater. Want to come see a show with me sometime?" I offered, sipping at what was left of my drink.

Rykiel folded his hands and rested his chin on them with a smirk. "Are you asking me out?"

I nearly inhaled my drink and began coughing. I knew he was joking but I was still taken by surprise.

"You're adorable, but I'm a married man, Leander. The wife might get jealous."

"It's not a date …"

"It's nice to know I've still got it." He winked at me. "Sure, I'll go. Just let me know when."

"All right." I breathed a sigh of relief. "She's not upset that I'm taking up so much of your time?"

He laughed. "I think she's glad you're giving her a break from me."

We finished up at the restaurant and parted with the promise to meet up again soon. That gave me about two or three weeks to do anything before I would hear from him again.

On the way home, my v-phone buzzed in my pocket. Dad had bought it for me for me on my birthday, and he'd gotten a new one for himself as well. It was a huge improvement over the outdated version at home. I could show Dad everything around me. He did the same with me, often showing me things that were going on at his camp.

I answered the phone with a smile, "Hi Dad."

"Hey there. What's going on?"

"I was just with Rykiel. I'm heading home now."

"Oh, how is he?"

"He was almost killed by a wesp." My voice didn't carry a hint of concern.

"Ah, I see. That does sound like Ryki." Dad followed suit. He knew Rykiel's dramatics well.

"What's up?"

"I just wanted to call you to let you know that I won't be able to call for a while. We're going on a mission," he answered seriously, "and I didn't want you to worry."

"How long?" I asked.

Everything about him sagged, from his expression to his posture. "We're hoping to be back in four weeks, but it could be as long as a month. Are you going to be okay?"

Twenty to twenty-seven days? I'd never gone so long without talking to him. The prospect was daunting but I didn't want to discourage him.

"Yeah, I'll be fine," I held my voice steady. "Is it dangerous?"

He shook his head as he answered, "Don't worry. We'll be fine. Have you gone to the employment office yet?"

"Not yet."

"You need to go in. Don't put it off too long."

"But I'm already making money," I countered.

"What have you been doing?"

"Just some odd jobs." It was partially true.

His disapproving tone leaked all over his carefully chosen words, "There's nothing wrong with odd jobs, but you should find something with reliable, steady pay."

"I'll look sometime. But I'm doing great, honest."

I wished I could tell him how well I was doing without raising his suspicions. I wasn't rich, but I was earning good chunks of money from the sales.

"That's fine. Just don't wait too long. Employers will wonder why you didn't start working sooner, and you want to find a job that interests you."

I already found a spot in something that interested me. Much more than anything at the employment office ever would.

"Don't worry about it. I've been making money," I reassured him.

He knitted his brows. "What exactly are you doing?"

"Finding stuff for people."

He tilted his head. "That's … different. You get paid to do that?"

"Yeah. I'm pretty good at it. I should open my own business!"

He dropped into silence, as he often did when he was mulling something over. I knew he didn't understand what I was doing or how I could earn money doing it, and that worried him.

"Hey," I leaned in, "do you want me to help pay for the house or something? I could help with the bills."

He smiled softly. "Don't worry about that. It's my house, I'll pay for it. You should save your money for when you get your own place."

It was a difficult balancing act. I wanted to help without raising his suspicions, but I could tell he didn't think I earned much. Surrendering for the moment, I decided to change the subject.

"All right. Hey, check this out." I pointed the v-phone towards a store. "They updated the entrance."

We chatted until I got home. My hand was on the doorknob when Dad said, "Well, I should probably get going. I'll talk to you in a few weeks."

My chest tightened suddenly. I did my best to beat down my anxiety and replied cheerfully, "Okay, be careful on your mission."

"I will. I love you."

After a quick scan of the area to see that I was alone, I answered back, "I love you, too."

He ended the connection. My stomach twisted. It would be the first time I went without talking to him for so long. The longest I'd ever gone without seeing him before was … a week? Perhaps. A whole month … That was a long time.

We didn't talk all day. A lot of times our conversations were brief, but knowing that I could always reach him gave me a sense of peace. Looking at the phone and knowing I couldn't call him was difficult to bear. Just the thought made me feel uncomfortably detached from him. Worse yet, I wouldn't know exactly where he was. He did say he'd be fine. I'd have to take his word for it.

As soon as I walked in, I grabbed a scrap of paper and sat at our desk, scribbling a calendar for the next month. It was the twenty-seventh of the fourth month, so tomorrow would be the first of the fifth month. I made a grid five squares wide and six squares high, then filled in the numbers for each day and pinned it up next to the desk. Tomorrow I could cross out the first day. Maybe I'd spend more time with Valli, or even Rykiel, and idly hoped that Ellora would give me something to do.

That done, I busied myself in the garden. I had replaced the plants for Dad before he arrived for my birthday. School had taught me enough about botany to do a decent job. I had cleaned the house and even picked up food, too. After everything that went wrong on his first visit I'd wanted him to see that I was taking care of things.

After gardening, I washed up and lay down on the couch. Life was relaxing since I graduated.

Since Dad paid for everything, I didn't have any bills to worry about. I earned money on Ellora's jobs, and even had the child support money from my mom transferred into my account when I hit nineteen. It hadn't been as much as I'd expected but, as Dad explained, when he moved to the capital he hadn't planned on paying for a home by himself on minimum wage. He couldn't afford to move, so he had to use the money to help pay bills sometimes. It didn't matter to me. It was a free pile of cash.

The money was accumulating. Dad even kept sending spending money. I felt badly about it, so I usually spent it on stuff for him.

When I wasn't out finding stuff for Ellora, I was hanging out with Valli. He invited me to auditions or shows often. Life was good, if a bit boring.

The beep of our home v-phone interrupted my thoughts. I knew it couldn't be Dad since he'd just called.

I rounded the couch and plopped down in front of the desk, bringing up the video. Ellora popped up on it.

"Hey." She started with her arms folded. She was leaning back in a chair with her body at an angle. The background was her room at the theater. It had bold pinks and purples, balanced out by white so that it wouldn't become overpowering.

"What is it?" I asked. *Please don't be Wilten Crags. Anything else is fine.*

"I have something that I think you'd like." She raised a brow and plastered a grin on her face.

She always had something good when she got smug. Or at least something profitable. That she thought I would *like* it was new. I tensed, hiding the anticipation in my voice, "Really? What is it?"

"You're going to have to come here to find out. I have some documents I need to give you, too," she explained.

Documents? I furrowed my brows. That was definitely new. Most of the time I just got directions and a lift from Galloughs.

"All right, when should I go over?"

"How about right now?"

I glanced back at the room. I wasn't doing anything in particular. "All right. I'll be there in a bit."

She flipped off the call without waiting for a good-bye.

I stretched before tossing my thin jacket back on, grabbing my bag, and heading to the theater. Ever since I met Valli, things had changed. I was almost a staple at the theater now.

Two guards stood at the entrance. One I recognized well – Aliseam. She was a large woman with cropped hair. The dull pink uniform suited her well. Next to her was a woman who had only been there a few months. A replacement for a guard who had died about half a year before, I assumed.

Aliseam's gaze flicked my direction and she waved me in without hesitation. I strolled through the lobby to the back. A deep maroon covered the walls and floor. Cloth posters of former and current plays lined the walls. Ellora appeared on a few of them.

A small hallway in the back attached the theater to the living quarters. It kept the maroon theme throughout. The living quarters had a lengthy hallway with eighteen rooms, nine on each side. They were divided into sections of four rooms separated by open areas with dining and recreational space, except for the end where six rooms shared a space.

I recognized many of the people who lived there now. As I walked through, I noticed Tenore's door was ajar. She was one of the technicians and their primary repair person. I had no doubt that she was engrossed in her work, surrounded by electronic parts.

At one of the tables an actor was having a drink. Seolian. She was one of the best known comedians in the theater. When I went to see Valli's plays, she usually played the best friend of the main character or whatever comic relief the play had. Her physique was somewhat lanky, and she always kept her hair short. She acknowledged me with a nod when I waved.

Ellora's room was at the end and to the right. The door opened promptly when I knocked. I moseyed over to her bed and sat on the edge of it with my hands shoved in my pockets. The bedspread was a dull pink with a lavender design on the bottom and opposite top

12

corner. The door closed with a click, giving us the privacy we needed.

"So what did you find?" I asked.

She grabbed papers off of her desk, holding them up. "Something far older than anything we've ever gotten before."

I shot upright. A genuine relic?

"Really? What is it?" my pitch heightened.

"You know how there are statues of the generals in front of the castle?"

"Yeah."

They stood in rows behind the front pillars, staring out at the world. I saw them often, whenever I passed by the castle.

"And how there used to be a different line of kings?" she continued.

I nodded, wondering what she was getting at.

"And, of course, you should know about General Luenlore."

"Yeah." I nodded again. Was it an item General Luenlore had owned?

"Well, way back when she was around, they used to have statues of the generals that came before her. Sometime after she killed the king and replaced him, those statues were destroyed." She smirked, smug in her delivery. "And I found out where one of them is."

I gawked at her. A statue like that would be over a thousand years old. It was truly a relic if there ever was one.

"Seriously?" I yelped. "Where?"

Her smirk faded. "That's the tough part. It's in Rhodaren."

"Rhodaren?" I blinked in surprise. "How did it get over there? And how did you find out about it?"

"I have no idea how it got there. But I found out from a contact I have in Cerna." She held the papers out to me. I took them and scanned over them. It looked like a copy of some sort of authentication form from Rhodaren. I flipped the page to see a vague map of Rhodaren with some areas marked off.

"How did someone in Cerna find out?" I asked. Even if she knew someone who would talk to Geuranians, that still wasn't enough. Rhodarens wouldn't live anywhere near Cerna.

"Someone I knew, knew a Geuranian in Cerna, who knew a Geuranian, who lives on the border of Geuran and Rhodaren, who in turn knew some Rhodarens …," she explained. It was a line of unlikely people all willing to talk to each other. It was hard enough to grasp Naggians and Geuranians talking without adding Rhodarens into the mix.

Still, I had met a Geuranian I liked before. I couldn't be the only one.

"What's this?" I held up the map.

"Someone took the statue in to be identified and authenticated. That map shows what city she took it to, so she must be near there somewhere." Ellora moved closer to me, pointing at the paperwork. "This has her name on it. You should be able to find her using this information."

"It's a start, at least," I agreed. A name and a place. All I needed was a ride to take me thousands of miles across enemy territory.

"Think you could handle it?" She cocked an eyebrow at me.

I looked up at her, hesitating before straightening up and answering confidently, "Sure, I handled Geuran." I paused, asking, "Did your contact have any way for me to get there?"

She shrugged. "That part is on you. I don't have anyone who'll drive through Geuran."

Hiding my misgivings, I nodded. There were three possible paths to Rhodaren: in the north we shared a border along a vast expanse of frozen mountains; Lyruna, the dense jungle, separated us in the center of the continent, and Geuran sat below Rhodaren to their south, blocking our path that way.

Traversing mountains in below freezing temperatures wasn't an option. Lyruna was known for its danger. Even plants attacked people there, and few who went in ever came back out. The only option left was Geuran.

If I sneaked onto a Geuranian vehicle going northwest until I reached the border they shared with Rhodaren to their north, I could work from there. I glanced down at the map. Only places in Rhodaren had been marked off, but it had a faint outline of the other two countries. Nagdecht took up a large portion of the eastern half of the continent. Lyruna was like a circle in the middle. On the western side were Geuran and Rhodaren, with Geuran taking up the smaller southern part and Rhodaren sitting above them. We had little contact with Rhodaren because of their location. Just getting there would likely be the most difficult part of the mission.

Dad was busy, and I didn't expect Rykiel to get in touch with me for a couple of weeks. That gave me time to get there, find the statue, and come back before anyone would notice I was missing.

"Great. Look over that paperwork and I'll arrange for Galloughs to get you to the border. You better figure out what supplies you're going to need." The smirk returned. "I'd suggest a jacket."

I huffed. Rhodaren was known for being a cold place. "No problem. I'll get back to you."

After I shoved the paperwork into my bag, I left her room, ready to head home, when the door to the next room opened. Valli stepped out, pausing in surprise when he saw me.

"Oh, Leander." He stopped, holding his door open. "What are you doing here?" He was wearing a silky purple dress with a vine of pink flowers decorating one side.

"I just stopped by to see Ellora. What are you doing?"

"I'm reading the next script and was about to get a drink. Want to come in? If you don't have anything else to do."

He stepped back, revealing his room. I smiled. I wasn't in a rush and his company was welcome. "Sure, I'm not busy at the moment."

"I'll grab us some drinks."

I waited in his room while he went to the nearest kitchen area. The white walls had pastel blue flowers decorating them. Papers were stacked on his desk next to a vase full of flowers I had given him and a lamp. His pillows had frills, and the bed had a curtain at the bottom. I plopped onto his chair, setting down my bag.

The blues in his room reminded me of my own room. I think Dad had expected me to turn out more like Valli, and as I grew up he waffled, unsure what I was going to like. He didn't know if he should get me the gentle blues and purples or the bolder pinks and whites. Then I subverted it all by wearing mostly browns and grays.

Valli came back with a small tray of drinks and a tiny pitcher. Considering the pale yellow color, the drinks were likely citrus. Pouring a cup, he slid it over to me.

"Anything new?" He sat down on his bed with a glass in his hand.

I hesitated. Should I tell him what Ellora and I were up to? He already knew I'd been to Geuran, and he had some idea that I didn't have a typical job. Morbid things like breaking into Wilten Crags didn't enter our conversations. I didn't let them. But he was fascinated by other countries, and since he found out about my visit to Geuran I became the de facto Geuranian expert. All questions about Geuran were directed to me and I knew the answers to almost none of them. Even so, the admiration I received for it was addictive.

"Actually," I grinned, "I'm going to go to Rhodaren." My end decision was to brag.

"What?" His eyes widened. "Really?" He leaned forward, his eyes scanning me before holding a hand over his mouth. "Aren't you scared?"

I watched his reaction with amusement and shrugged. "It's just Rhodaren. How bad can it be?"

Nagdecht didn't interact with Rhodaren, but we still knew about them. They weren't hostile like Geuran. They were lazy, sickly people with a do-nothing government. It would take a microscope to find their army, and their technology was so outdated they might not even have microscopes. They didn't inspire the fear that Geuranians could.

"But you still have to go through Geuran to get there, don't you?" He sounded breathless.

I feigned confidence. "Yeah, but I've been there before. I'm sure I can get through no problem." At least I could impress Valli. Ellora was never awed. The longer I worked with her, the more I found myself talking to Valli afterward to boost my ego.

Taking a sip, I relaxed, leaning against his desk as I sat sideways in the chair. A sharp, tangy flavor rolled over my tongue. They kept the good stuff around here – it tasted great.

"I'd still be scared. I could never do something like that." He settled down, his hand lowering from his mouth. "How are you going to get there?"

18

"I'm not sure yet, I haven't had much time to think about it. But I'm guessing I'll sneak onto a truck in Geuran or something like that. Then I'll have to figure out something in Rhodaren."

"That sounds so dangerous. Are you sure it's worth it?" he asked.

I laughed. "It's to get back a piece of our history. I'm sure I'll be fine."

Valli worried and I reassured him until we stumbled onto a different topic. We played some cards until he needed to go to rehearsal, then I went home to study the documents.

I ended the day by writing a note for Rykiel, explaining that I was visiting friends and I'd call him back in a few days. By the time he visited, it would already be about two weeks, and with the note I could probably squeeze out another week without him worrying. That done, I went to bed.

3
5, 1, 3399
Windsday

She approached the entrance of a seedy bar. Dusk claimed the land, and only the dim glow of outside lights made it possible to see. In her youth, she had only been to a few bars, and always with friends. Many of those friends were gone now. Moved away or departed. Now she stood outside alone with only the strength to walk.

After she pushed through the doors, her eyes roamed the inside. Many young people were gathered around. Some flirting, some drinking, some playing. The bar had a pair of billiards tables to the side. Five people were playing on them, carefully knocking their opponents' balls into pins to deduct points while trying to hit the positive pins with their own balls. She could hear one of the women laughing. "Oh, don't you even think of hitting my ball! I know where you sleep." Others taunted the woman at play to do it.

Walking through the bar was like a dream. She had never imagined herself in this position. With every step, she moved further into another world. Her cane hit the floor with a thump when she stopped at the counter. The barkeep tended to other patrons before moving over to her.

"How can I help you?" She had a smooth, clean look, with hair pulled to one side and strong arms. The sleeves of her starched white shirt were rolled up, and black pants completed the look of a not-quite uniform.

"Would it be possible to speak in the back?"

The woman raised an eyebrow, hesitating before answering plainly, "Yeah, sure. Just head over there." She nodded her head towards a hallway. "Second door to the left, I'll be there in a couple minutes."

The hallway was dark. If someone were to attack her, she would be trapped, she realized. It was a risk coming to a place like this and relying on someone else to lead her honestly. She walked into the room the woman had indicated. Its furnishings were a plain table and a few mismatched chairs. Taking a seat, she folded her hands on the tabletop and waited. It was dark and quiet.

The woman came into the room and stood with a hand on her hip. "What is it you're looking for?"

"I'd like to purchase a gun. Do you know where I can get one?"

"Have you ever used a gun before?"

"No."

"I'm not sure I'd recommend you start getting into guns. It takes some training to get used to them, and recoil can be pretty nasty. If you don't know what you're doing you can accidentally shoot your own head off."

"I know. But I need one," she repeated, patiently.

The woman seemed hesitant, but gave in with sigh, "I can help you out. Do you have the money for one?"

"Money won't be a problem."

4
5, 1, 3399
Windsday

The morning both dragged on and flew by. As I packed my things, I constantly felt like there should be more for me to do. I grabbed everything I could think of, from a compass to food. My jacket was on. I paced the house, continuously stopping in front of my bag again to reassess my choices.

Excitement was bubbling up inside of me. Soon, I'd be in another country again. It was hard to believe it had already been two years since I went to Geuran. A smile crept onto my face. Deckard was still over there somewhere.

I beat the thought away. Deckard was in Geuran along with thirty million other Geuranians. The last I'd heard from him was a couple of years ago when he said he was going to a northern camp for a while. I didn't know what camp, or if he'd even still be there. My chances of finding him were low to non-existent – yet the possibility nagged at my mind.

The doorbell broke the silence. I was supposed to go meet Galloughs at his bar. I wasn't expecting anyone to come over.

I opened the door to Valli. Some sort of brown clothing hung over his arm. It contrasted greatly with the navy blue he was wearing.

"Valli! What are you doing here?"

"I was hoping I had the right house." He held up an arm, offering the piece of clothing to me. "I brought this for you."

Gently lifting the coat, I held it up. It hung all the way down to my knees. The fabric was heavier and thicker than my jacket.

As I examined it he continued timidly, "I thought you might need it."

I folded it and hung it over my arm, meeting his eyes again with a smile. "Thanks."

"Is it all right?"

"It looks great." I stepped back. "Did you want to come in or anything?"

"No, no, I'm fine." He held his hands up. "I just thought you probably didn't have a lot of clothes for cold weather."

He was right. The capital didn't have cold weather the way they did up north.

I shrugged off my jacket and folded it, putting on the coat to show him I'd wear it. In seconds, I already felt extra-warm. As I tugged it into place I looked back up at him. His eyes had a spark of life in them. I flashed him a grin.

"When are you going to be leaving?"

"Actually, I should be heading out now."

Grabbing my bag, I shoved my jacket into it and stepped out of my house. I locked the door and left the note for Rykiel to find. When I turned to Valli, I hesitated, unsure what to say.

"You'll be careful, won't you?" he asked in a hushed tone. He wrung and twisted the end of his sleeve as if he was hoping to squeeze the dye right out of it.

"Don't worry, I'll be fine," I reassured him. "I'll see you when I get back."

We walked to the corner where I boarded a cart. With a wave, we parted. It was considerate of him to bring me something. I'd have to pay him back later.

5

"You can still turn back, you know. You don't have to go through with this."

I sat by Galloughs as he drove me towards the Geuranian border. Discouraging me was a favorite pastime of his, but this time he seemed genuinely concerned. I could understand why. Skipping hundreds of miles through Geuran wouldn't be a simple task.

Still, this was a find unlike any other. I glanced down at the papers. They had details about the statue – or what was left of it. Just like Ellora said, the statue had been destroyed. The only part of the statue brought to the appraiser was the remains of a hollow bust. The insides were filthy and the outside was eroded.

At least that would be easier to carry back than a full statue. There was no information about who the model was. Rhodarens probably didn't know our generals. It was so old, we might not even be able to tell anymore. Information from that era was sketchy at best.

"I'm fine. Besides, I can't pass this up. The chances I'll ever get to find anything like this again are slim to none." I covered my anxiety. I was convincing myself as much as I was him.

"Just because you got out of Geuran before doesn't mean it's not dangerous," he warned me. "Don't get cocky, Son."

I folded my arms and stared straight ahead. "I *know* that."

He glanced at me, then looked back out the window.

"You don't have to prove anything, you know," he said. "You can head back home. There are other things for you to do."

"Do you think Tevias would run away?" I challenged him.

"Tevias died young, Son," he answered bluntly. That quieted me. Tevias disappeared at around twenty-nine, never to be seen or heard from again.

I mulled over Geuran. Last time I'd been there, it was definitely scary, but I had met Deckard. It was hard to believe two years had gone by. The chance I would hitch a ride on the same vehicle he was driving was near non-existent, and yet I couldn't help playing the scenario over and over in my head. That small possibility that I might get to catch up with him was almost worth the risk by itself. I found myself thinking about that more than the statue.

"You've got your dad. You graduated recently. You've got plenty you can do," he continued.

I appreciated what he was trying to do. For all our bickering in the past few years, he was trying to convince me to stay home for my own safety. It was tempting. If I stayed home, there'd be no worries.

But that meant no chance of Deckard. And the statue ... The statue was truly something on par with what Tevias would find. This one item could bring me fame like no other. It belonged in a museum, just like the items Tevias had found. I hadn't matched his collection yet. Even if I found the statue, it would just be that and the flute that I had found.

My eyes focused on the hem of my sleeve as my fingers played with it. Then there was Valli ... He'd even bought me a coat for my adventure. How could I go back and tell him I was too scared to do it? I wanted to be the adventurer he thought I was, not some kid who stumbled over the border once. What would I do if I turned back? I could already hear what Ellora would say. It would be scavenger missions for the rest of my life, and if I complained, she would remind me that I'd been too frightened to find relics when I had the chance. I would see Valli's disappointed face. He would never say anything, but I would see it in his eyes, and somehow that hurt even more than anything Ellora would say.

"I'm going to go through with this," I said, more determined. I stared straight ahead. Galloughs eyes sat on me for a moment, lips pressed tightly together before turning ahead. We rode the rest of the way in silence.

Galloughs dropped me off near the border. He lingered in his truck for awhile. I sensed that he was waiting for me to change my mind. The temptation was there, but I resisted it and forged ahead. First, I needed to get near Geuranian civilization. Then I had to find a vehicle that was headed towards Rhodaren. That meant going west and staying as far north as possible.

I walked. I walked until my legs ached, but after a few hours I saw the signs of a military camp in the distance. As soon as I saw it, I got low to the ground and crept forward. When I found a large bush, I forced my way inside of it so I would be hidden from all sides. The branches grabbed and scraped me but I brushed it off.

Geuranians patrolled around the camp. There was no way I could skip around during the day. I needed to wait until night.

With that in mind, I ate something and lay down, using my pack as a pillow until evening came. As soon as the sky began turning purple, I brushed off and crawled towards the camp. They still had lights on, but there were many dark spots to hide in.

I crawled behind one of the buildings, peeking around the corner. The sounds of people murmuring drifted around the camp, but I didn't see anyone. I made my way around until I found where they parked the trucks.

Now I just needed to find out where they were going. But how?

Would they already be loaded? I checked for soldiers before opening the back of a truck. It was filled with ammunition crates. Probably not headed towards Rhodaren – they weren't at war with Rhodaren. I closed it and checked the next one, going through them until I found one that was loaded with smaller boxes and letters. Curious, I examined a box.

Packages they were sending home? I read over the addresses and wished I had a better grasp of Geuranian geography. I was good at remembering places but we didn't study Geuran much in school. After looking through a dozen, one address seemed familiar. It sounded like a place that I recalled seeing closer to the north of their maps.

Perhaps the truck would be making a round there sometime. If I hitched a ride I could hop off when it was close. But how would I hide? I couldn't stay inside the truck. They'd be opening it up all of the time. There was no way to ride the bottom of the truck without my skin being scraped off.

I glanced up. The top of the truck had a small railing around it, and leather straps. Placing one of the boxes on top, I hopped down to take a look. The truck was high enough that I didn't see the box from the ground. If I lay low, and in the middle, no one would notice me.

After putting the box back and closing the truck, I climbed on the top and lay down. Nothing else was on top of it save for the loose straps that were connected to the bars. Large items were obviously

28

loaded on top sometimes, but not at the moment. I tied two of the straps together to form a barrier in front of the ladder. There was a gap in the bars there and I didn't want to slide through it.

Zipping up my coat, I used my bag as a pillow and went to sleep.

I woke with a start. The truck lurched forward. It accelerated and I slid down the roof towards the small opening in the bars. My clothes scraped along the metal. Barely conscious of what was happening, I grabbed at the roof because of instinct alone.

My legs slipped under the leather straps in the back. When I pushed myself up with my arms the rest of my body flipped over the straps. In a blur I flipped over backwards and was about to fall off the truck head first.

Something caught my ankle and clamped down on it. I yelled thoughtlessly, screaming as the truck moved while I hung upside-down on the back, my ankle caught in a strap. The truck stopped and I smacked into the doors. Wobbling about, I flailed my arms but there was nothing for me to grab.

"What the …?"

I heard the bewildered voice but I didn't care who it came from.

"Get me down from here!" I shouted. My leg ached from the strain. Hands grabbed me and lifted me up, but no matter how much they tugged my ankle was caught. A third person hopped onto the back of the truck, fiddling with the straps until I was loose. The lower half of my body hit the ground as my upper half was held up. Dirt flew into the air and I struggled to stand. My leg tingled in a half-asleep state.

I glanced around. A whole camp of soldiers had stopped in their tracks to stare at me. Three men stood around me. Not a Deckard among them. The only

29

reason I wasn't pinned to the ground seemed to be because they were so baffled.

"All right, it was a stupid idea!" I yelled at them. Their bewilderment evaporated and they finally became capable of movement again. Some chuckled, others looked around for answers.

That didn't last long. In seconds, I was dragged away.

6
5, 2, 3399
Firsday

I paced the cell. I'd escaped a Geuranian jail before; I'd just have to find a way to do it again. This one was sturdy. The ground was concrete. The walls were solid, and the bars set firmly into the ground and ceiling.

One soldier guarded me. He sat on a chair across from my cell, leaning against some of the bars with his feet up on a stool. Mine was the only occupied cell, so he didn't have a lot to watch, and I got the feeling he was staring at me. With a sigh I stopped and placed my hands on my hips. How would I do this? I needed to get the keys somehow. *Maybe if I fake an injury …* Just feet from my reach, the keys hanging from his belt were taunting me.

Suddenly, he sat straight up in the chair. His feet hit the ground with a thud. He got up, stretched, and headed for the door.

Getting as close as I could to the bars, I watched the new guard come in and accept the keys. Just a bit taller than me, a little on the skinny side, lazy movements, hair that attempted to curl even though it was buzzed … *Deckard!*

My heart skipped a beat. The first guard hid his yawn with a hand as he left, leaving me alone with his replacement.

I stared wide-eyed at his goofy smirk.

"So it *was* you," he said.

I couldn't believe it. Trying to hide my shock, I answered as flippantly as I could but it came off stilted, "I hardly recognized you. You all kind of look alike …"

"Well, if you're going to be that way." He spun around and made as if he was going to leave.

"I recognized you, I recognized you!" I grabbed the bars. "Now get over here and help me out!"

He sauntered over, propping himself up against the wall next to my cell, his voice high. "I don't know. I could get in trouble." His argument only convinced me that he still liked to joke around.

"How did you know I was in here?" I struggled to keep my voice steady.

"I drove here about noon and heard rumors that a stupid Nadder got caught hanging upside-down off the back of a truck." He placed a hand over his heart. "And I thought of you."

After all my daydreaming, I wasn't the one who found him; he found me. Still, I grimaced at the strange word he used for us. I had an immediate distaste for it.

"Naggian," I corrected him.

"What's that?"

"That's what we're called. Naggians."

"First time I've heard that one." He shrugged. "All right."

"I'm surprised you aren't in here with me," I joked, raising an eyebrow at him. I joined him leaning on the bars, with my chest pressed against them and my arms hanging out.

"I've cleaned up." He held one of his wrists behind his back. "I haven't been locked up in almost a year."

"Really?"

"Aren't you the one who suggested I clean up my act?" He smirked at me.

"Well, yeah, but I'm surprised you actually did it," I fumbled for the words to explain myself and moved on, "Anyway, I need help out."

"What are you going after this time? A piccolo?"

"No, a statue."

"Sounds big. Where's it supposed to be?"

"Rhodaren."

"Rhodaren?" he raised his voice. He gave me an incredulous look. "That's a long way away from here."

"I know. It would help if I could hitch a ride there," I hinted ever so subtly.

"Are you suggesting," he placed a hand to his chest acting thoroughly appalled, "I help sneak an enemy across the country?"

"No, just me." I mugged for him.

He smirked, glancing away. "I don't know ... I've been a pretty good soldier."

"Have you really?" I probed.

"Well, I've stayed out of trouble."

I nudged his shoulder through the bars. "Are you going to help me or not?"

He lulled his head to one side as if he was mulling over a difficult question, and looked back with a grin on his face.

"Then hurry up and get me out!" I pushed his shoulder some more, bouncing in place.

"All right, all right, give me a minute." He pulled away and paced in front of the cell. "If I volunteered to do one of the long drives they probably wouldn't suspect me of anything. No one is going to think a Nadder is heading to Rhodaren ..."

"Naggian," I corrected.

"All right, Naggian." He shrugged. "Should be easy enough to get one of those jobs. Most people try to avoid the long drives. Long hours for not much more pay."

"Great, then let's go!"

"We still have to get you out of there."

That had become a secondary thought.

"Can't you just unlock it?" I asked.

He leaned against the bars right in front of me, his arms hanging through. I leaned back as his face got close to mine. "That would make it kind of obvious I let you out, wouldn't it?"

"Yeah." I knitted my brows. "But, what else are we going to do?"

He laid an arm flat across the bars.

"How about this: I give you the key and find out who is guarding you later. I get him drunk before he heads down here. He falls asleep, you escape and meet me at the trucks."

I nodded, but paused. "What if he doesn't fall asleep?" I didn't want him driving off without me. It was hard to express how relieved I was to have him.

"Then I pretend to have engine troubles."

I smiled. Escape had gone from difficult to a sure thing. In a matter of minutes, the toughest part of my trip had become the easiest. Getting the statue would be a cinch.

"Here." He pulled off one of the keys and handed it to me. I slipped it in my pocket.

A thought hit me. "Deckard, do you think you could get my stuff back?"

"Sure, there was nothing important in there so they dumped it in the lost and found."

"What?" I stiffened. I didn't like the thought of people digging through my things. "Are you sure?"

"Yeah, I checked it first when I thought it might be you. Signed up for guard duty later."

"Did you get it out?"

He quieted. After a few moments he spoke up again, hesitantly, "Yeah, well. When I thought it might be yours I took it."

I breathed a sigh of relief. At least I would get my stuff back.

Time passed by faster after that. I relaxed on the bed and we idly chatted while waiting for his shift to

34

be over. As the end neared, we quieted. He didn't want anyone to walk in and catch us talking to each other.

Finally, he stood as another soldier came into the room. He glanced at me. It felt strange that I couldn't say good-bye to him, but I watched him leave.

It was just a wait for the guard after this one. I stared at the gray ceiling from my bed.

At least my stupid display had been good for something. Word had gotten out and Deckard found me because of it. A smile sneaked onto my face before I realized it.

Time slogged along until the next guard finally came. His movements were sluggish. Leaning back in the seat, he put his feet up and tilted his head back with his arms resting across his stomach. Staying discreet, I kept an eye on him. He moved so little I wasn't sure if he was asleep or not.

I racked my mind for a question, and spoke up quietly in case he was asleep, "Hey? I need to go to the bathroom, can I have a little privacy?"

No response. I swung my legs off the bed and leaned forward.

"Geuranians are stupid."

Still no answer. I tiptoed towards the door and reached through the bars, using the key Deckard had given me earlier. It took some time to wiggle it into the keyhole and turn it. I stayed as quiet as I could with the key clinking and scraping against the metal.

I shuddered when the door squealed open, pausing to gauge the guard's reaction. He didn't move, and bit by bit, I opened it farther and spun around to the other side. I shut it quietly and crept towards the exit.

When I opened the exit door a hair, the evening sky greeted me. It was pink, going on purple. I could hear people around the middle of the camp. It sounded like they were gathered together as a group – maybe eating – which gave me an opportunity to make a run to the trucks.

Running through the camp when it was still light enough to see was disconcerting, but I ducked behind anything that provided adequate cover and kept away from the noise. Finally, I reached the trucks. Hiding behind a nearby building, I watched the area until I felt sure Deckard was the only one around. He was packing some crates into the back of a truck by himself.

I approached, my eyes still scouring everything around me. "Aren't those heavy?"

He glanced at me as he slid one up. "They're empty. They'll be filled up and be sent back."

"Oh." I nodded. "Where should I go?"

"Just duck down in the front seat."

The door was already open. I climbed over the driver seat, sitting on the floor in front of the passenger side, and tucked my knees up to my chest. Before long, he joined me. He slammed the driver side door shut. The truck rumbled, vibrating and pushing forward. When it was safe he waved for me to get up and I climbed onto the chair.

We had a long drive to Rhodaren. Finally, an opportunity to get to know Deckard better. We last saw each other so briefly, there was little time for pleasantries back then.

But where to start? I glanced at him. One hand was on the wheel while the other was slung over the back of the seat. The seats were fused together like a couch.

"So," I started off, "who taught you to drive?" Learning to drive was unusual and Deckard didn't seem the motivated type.

He glanced my way with a smirk and an amused huff. "No one."

I knitted my brows. "What do you mean?"

"Well," he tilted his head back and forth in a bouncy movement, "the truth is I may have fudged my résumé a bit."

I shouldn't have been surprised but somehow I was.

"So you lied and said you could drive? Why?"

"I needed to put something down so I wouldn't be sent to Lyruna."

It was a true. A smart-mouthed destructive soldier like Deckard would have been shipped off to Lyruna in a heartbeat, and people didn't come back from Lyruna.

"But how did you keep from being caught?"

"I faked it until I figured it out." He paused to chuckle. "They got pretty pissed at some of the first driving jobs I did. A tire blew out and I tried to fix it. I heard about the hole I made in that truck for weeks."

Yet he was still laughing about it. I couldn't help but smile. He was hopeless.

"What about your family?"

His eyes flicked my way a couple of times, as if for once he was thinking something over. Finally, he cracked an odd smile and said, "My dad got crushed by a cart."

Was he being serious? I didn't know if I was supposed to laugh or not.

"... Really?"

"Yeah, it was a freak accident," he answered without a care.

I winced. Somehow the news seemed to cause me more pain than him. "I'm sorry."

"It's no big deal. It happened when I was little, I don't really remember him."

That explained how he could be so disconnected.

He continued, "My mom married my step-dad after a while. Big military man. We never got on very well, since I wasn't his and all. Eventually they had kids and I didn't really fit in anymore." I watched as Deckard spoke. He acted as if it had no effect on him, but his façade had cracks in it. His expression became serious for a moment, and as hard as he tried to keep his voice even, it trembled. He shrugged and kept his eyes averted.

"What about your mom?"

"I know she loves me." He shrugged. "Guess she just wanted the whole husband and kids thing more."

An odd silence fell over us. He peered at me with a smarmy expression. "I actually put off joining the army a few years just to piss him off. Thought about joining the whole Peace thing, but, you know."

"'Peace thing'?"

"Yeah, the Peace Troupe. They're a charity organization. Lots of people join it when they want to put off going into the army for a while, because people can't complain that you're doing charity work."

It didn't sound bad, so ... "Why didn't you want to join, then?"

"Because you're supposed to stay chaste while you're with them." He wrinkled his nose at the thought.

"So?" I pursed my lips, more demanding than I meant to be.

"Well, I didn't want to do *that*."

"It's not *that* bad."

Although I'd thought about it often enough, I was a busy person and I hadn't met anyone I wanted to be with yet. I didn't worry too much about it.

"So you've never ..." A wondering glance came my way before he blew the whole thing off with a sweep of his hand. "Never mind."

"It's not a big deal. I just haven't met anyone yet. You have?"

"Eh, I've been with a few people. Nothing serious." He chuckled. "Actually, there was a pibby

39

sleeping next to me at that camp. I barely got any sleep with all the noise he made."

"Oh?" I quirked a brow. The only thing the term brought to mind was a tiny, fuzzy animal, and it didn't seem like the Geuranian army would be that desperate for recruits.

"He even tried to convince me to do his work once. Like I'm going to do all the work during the day and night." He snorted.

I stared at him as I tried to figure out what he was talking about. He glanced towards me, and seeing my expression he continued, more furtive, "I didn't do it."

"Do what?"

"Sleep with him."

"Wait, what? What's a pibby?"

"You don't know?"

I shook my head.

"Oh," he relaxed, "they're the soldiers who sleep with other soldiers to get them to do their work."

"There's people like that?" I asked.

"Sure. I've never been interested in that sort of thing, though," he reassured me. "I don't need to pay to sleep with someone."

"I wouldn't want to do that, either. Did a lot of people there do it?"

It was the most openly I'd ever talked about sex. I was uncomfortable but curious.

"I wouldn't say 'a lot,' but there were definitely takers. It was annoying."

"And they don't get in trouble for doing that?"

"Eh, I doubt the captains would like it, but no one really says anything about it in a lot of the camps. Frankly, I think some of our superiors partake, too."

"I've never dealt with something like that."

"It's going to be a long, boring drive. If you want, I can sit here and scream next to you to replicate the experience," he offered mockingly. With a huff, I shook my head.

I pulled my coat on tighter. The front seat looked large enough for three people. I lay down on it. It was uncomfortably tight, but I didn't want to lie on top of Deckard. I curled up in a fetal position with the seat belt wrapped around my abdomen and over my chest.

Deckard reached into his jacket pocket and pulled out a bag of chips, holding it over me. "Want a snack?"

I tilted my head up. "You keep food on you?"

"I like to keep something around. I tend to get the munchies in the middle of the night."

Inspecting one briefly, I popped it in my mouth. They were salty and crunchy, but worked well enough for getting something into my stomach.

I didn't rest well. With how cramped I was and the constant rumbling of the engine, as well as my racing thoughts, I couldn't seem to fall asleep. Every now and then, the thought that I was going through Geuran flitted through my mind and my adrenaline pumped. Each passing second, I was getting farther and farther from Nagdecht.

Deckard made a pit stop, dropping me off before going into the cities and coming back for me. He brought back food and we set up a picnic outside the truck. Plopping down, I tried some of the food he brought first. It wasn't bad, but the bread that he was using was almost tasteless.

"What kind of bread is this?" I asked.

"Hmm? I dunno, just normal bread?"

I tugged my bag next to me. "You have to try some of our bread! I brought part of a loaf to snack on the first day."

Excited to share something from Nagdecht with him, I was shocked when I dug into the bag. It wasn't as intact as I had believed. A bunch of my food was missing, as well as my compass.

"They took my stuff!"

"I didn't get to it until around noon. Some of the guys were probably curious." Deckard didn't seem worried, but I was disappointed. I wanted to show him how good our food was and the rest of the food I had left I'd chosen for its longevity, not because it tasted great. He slid a sandwich over to me. Judging by his expression, he thought I was upset about not having something to eat.

Ears lowered, I accepted it, mumbling, "You would have liked it. Maybe when we come back I can get some more somehow."

"Don't worry about it. We can pick up plenty of food here."

"Yeah, but I wanted to show you some of *our* food. We have great food."

"Well, don't you have anything else?"

"Nothing good. I didn't want to pack a lot of stuff that would go bad." Staring at the bag, I came up with an idea. "Maybe when we come back we can stop by Cerna or something, and I can bring some back for you. It would be worth the wait!"

"Sure, whatever you want to do." He chuckled. "This bread better live up to its reputation."

With that settled, I felt better. I'd get a chance to share with him after all. Thoughts of hanging out in Cerna poured through my mind. Then I thought of the couple I had seen there years before. A Geuranian and a Naggian walking together ... but everyone else avoided them. They got dirty glares and some people even walked farther away to avoid them. Maybe Deckard and I could find a quiet spot to hang out somewhere.

Saving my rations, I feasted on the Geuranian food. It didn't quite live up to Naggian cuisine, but it was decent enough.

After that we packed up and continued on in the truck. Purple coated the sky and then shone a light blue again. The days of driving were long, and being stuck in a small space made it difficult to get comfortable. I appreciated the moments that Deckard left me somewhere. I could stretch out.

Another day dragged by with nothing to look at but expansive fields of grass. By the time night came, I managed to sleep because of boredom alone.

7

5, 5, 3399
Waddersday

Eventually dawn arrived and the sun shone brightly through the windshield. It was hard to believe two days had gone by. Deckard pulled to a stop in the middle of nowhere. The only things around were grass, bushes and a couple of trees.

"I'm going to go drop off the supplies and come back here. Just stay hidden until I get back," he explained.

"All right," I answered. Every limb ached when I climbed out of the truck. I plopped down in the grass, looking up at the trees. The rumbling of the truck grew distant. I was grateful for the break. Now I understood why few people volunteered for the long drives.

About an hour later, Deckard returned. I boarded again when he pulled to a stop, and we were off towards the Rhodaren border. Time seemed to slow to a crawl. Feeling jittery, my leg bounced up and down of its own accord.

After a while he parked near a tree. I hopped out and Deckard came around to join me. This was it.

Strapping my bag to my back, I looked at Deckard. "All right, we'll have to figure out how to meet up later."

"What do you mean?" he asked.

"Well, I'll have to figure out how many days you should give me before I come back here to get picked up ..."

"I'm going, too."

"You are?" I stared at him.

"Yeah."

"Are you sure? A Naggian is already going to stick out, but a Naggian and a Geuranian …"

"Eh." He shrugged, holding his hands out. "What can I say? You're a bad influence."

"*I'm* a bad influence?" my tone fluctuated.

"Yeah. I've been staying out of trouble for almost a year straight, and you come around and look what happens. I'm breaking a Nad- a Naggian out of prison and sneaking him across Geuran."

I huffed. "You were already in prison when we met, remember?"

He smirked, tapping his temple. "That should have been my first clue you were trouble."

I leered at him as he looked at me from the corner of his half-lidded eyes, eyebrows raised. Letting out a sigh, I rolled my eyes, smiling.

"Anyway," I changed the subject, "shouldn't we take the truck in, then?"

"No way. It's a Geuranian military vehicle. They'd notice it quick. We should go on foot."

"It's just Rhodarens, though. How bad could it be?"

Deckard gave me an odd look. "Rhodarens can be a lot of trouble."

"But they barely even have an army and it's not that big of a country."

"It's a huge country."

I furrowed my brows before realizing that Rhodaren was a third of the size of Nagdecht, but Geuran was around one tenth the size of our country. To them, Rhodaren would be large. Still, they weren't hostile like Geuran. I had trouble picturing them as scarier than Geuranians.

I turned towards the empty plains. "So this is the border?"

"Sort of."

"Sort of?"

46

"A while back, we won a war against them. But they're stubborn. They keep trying to claim this land is still theirs. There're problems around the border all the time because of it."

So the Rhodarens had Geuranian problems as well. It wasn't surprising. I sympathized with the Rhodarens.

He opened the truck on the passenger side and pulled out his pack, reaching in to slide his rifle out. He lifted it over his shoulder, ready to hook it onto his back.

"What are you doing?" I stopped him. Sometimes I forgot that he was a soldier.

"What?" he asked, confused.

"You can't take that with us!" I snapped.

He glanced at the rifle. "This? It's just in case something goes wrong."

"No way! I don't want to shoot anyone!" I insisted.

"I don't plan on shooting anyone, but if we get into trouble ..."

"No," I pointed at the truck, "you're leaving that here. Hide it in the truck or something."

I refused to accept it. Guns meant one thing. I wasn't a Rhodaren fan but I didn't intend to go in and hurt anyone. Bringing a rifle invited danger.

"All right, I won't bring it," he answered, exasperated, as he leaned into the truck and stashed it away. "But if things go bad it's on you," he warned me, though his voice stayed light.

We began our trek north on foot. Having grown up close to the border, Deckard had an idea where one of their towns would be. The chill in the air reminded me of Woodlor. It was farther north than I was used to. I rubbed my arms to keep myself warm as we walked, thankful for my new coat.

I sized him up as we went.

"Didn't you used to be bigger?" I finally asked. I recalled not meeting him eye to eye before.

"Pretty sure you just used to be smaller. I haven't grown in years," he answered.

I hummed curiously in response.

The first signs of life were in the form of a cottage in the middle of the countryside. It was one story and looked like a log cabin, but it was more like it was styled that way rather than an authentic log cabin. The wood was too crisp and smooth, like paneling. Garments flapped in the wind on a clothesline outside.

It fit the image I had of Rhodarens. From everything I'd read about them, they seemed like simple country folk.

"Let's sneak by," I suggested. His hand rested on my arm.

"Wait, I'm going to see who lives here."

"What? Why?"

"It could be a Geuranian home. I could ask for a snack or something if it is."

"Wait, isn't this Rhodaren?"

"Like I said, border issues. But even if it is a Rhodaren home, I'll probably be okay. I doubt I'm the first Geuranian to wander this far north."

I ducked behind a tree while Deckard approached the home. He circled the perimeter, never leaving my sight before he came back.

"It's Rhodarens. There's one on the other side of the house."

"I guess we can't expect any help then."

"Come on, we'll keep heading north."

Being close to a Rhodaren, I wanted to get a look, but we were too far. I could only see the silhouette of a person gardening outside.

The next sign of civilization came much later in a much different form. The outskirts of a city. A few buildings were in the distance. Slightly above them were the rails for their cart system. It wasn't like ours. Instead of having a rail on each side of a cart it looked like the carts hung off of one bar. How stable were they compared to ours?

One building looked like a convenience store with a wooden sign and lights in front. Another appeared to be a residence surrounded by shrubbery. They were all one story tall. Figures moved in the distance as people went about their business.

Deckard and I settled down and made a pseudo-picnic as we waited for evening to fall. Splitting up the food we brought, we tried some more of each other's cuisine. Geuranian food mostly seemed salty if anything, with things like chips and sandwiches with pickles in them. The foods I brought all had a longer shelf life than normal, so I only had things like hard fruits and foods that came in sealable packaging. Upon a second taste test, I determined Geuranian bread didn't compare to our bread. I couldn't wait to share a fresh loaf of the real thing with him. He had no idea what he was missing.

When darkness fell, we headed in. A rail system meant access panels, so we searched for the nearest one and hustled to avoid being noticed.

I was both grateful and worried when we found the first panel. The faint glow of the machine lit up my face when I stood in front of it. Waving Deckard to stay back, I pulled up my coat to try and give myself more cover. My hair, at least, was black, and my skin a light brown. On top of that, Rhodarens would never expect to see a Naggian here. It would be better for me to be spotted than him. Even if I didn't fit in, I didn't stick out as much.

When I went through the options I couldn't find anything but directions. No matter what I clicked on, I couldn't bring up their news, or information, or anything.

"How are you supposed to work these things?" I whispered to Deckard.

"I don't know. I've never been here."

I gave up and checked the maps against the papers I had. Comparing them, I noted our location and the location where the statue had been appraised.

"We need to head northeast," I whispered to him as I marked the map.

A second attempt to find their information failed. We were going to have to find it some other way, but how? How did Rhodarens look up people? Their system was confusing and didn't seem to dole out anything but directions.

"All right. How far is it?"

"I think we'll need to hitch a ride. Come on, let's get away from this light, I can't find anything else."

We ducked down in an alley next to one of the buildings. My nose felt like it was frozen. I put a hand to my mouth to blow some warm air on it. My breath came out as a fine fog. This cold was too much to sleep outside.

"We need to find somewhere warm to sleep. It's cold out here!"

"Well, it *is* Rhodaren."

"We need somewhere warm to rest and some way that we can get driven northeast." I rubbed my arms frantically. The coat helped, but wasn't enough to keep the cold at bay. I envied the people inside the buildings. They must have developed great heating systems here.

"Where can we go that's warm that we wouldn't be caught immediately?" Deckard asked.

"Just think. What's someplace that isn't always checked or occupied?"

"Shouldn't we just see if we can find a postal service or something? We need to hitch a ride. We're going to be in a bad spot if we're still stuck here in the morning."

"Wait, that's it. The postal service is probably closed by now. Maybe we can stay there for the night and use one of their trucks in the morning."

"How?"

"We'll figure it out later. Let's just see if we can find a place."

I was ready to rush back over to the access panel when I motioned for Deckard to stay. It would be better if only I went.

If nothing else, the panel did have directions. While I was looking the rails creaked. A cart whizzed by, the entire thing held up by the top middle. I hadn't noticed before, but in front of me a second rail curved down to bring it lower to the ground. I ducked my head quickly to hide my face as it went by. It didn't stop, passing by the alternative path and whizzing past. That seemed an odd way to do it.

Memorizing some directions, I grabbed Deckard and led him towards the post office, avoiding streets with too much light. We picked ones that didn't have their windows lit up. Some were so dark I could hardly tell where we were going. I'd never walked a pitch-black street before. It was a little frightening.

Trying to navigate when I could barely see my own hand took extra time, but we made our way to the little post office. The outside was unassuming. In the dark, I couldn't be sure what color it was, but I could make out the large, wall-sized windows in the front. The doors were glass and the walls had a crisscross paneling design on the front bottom half.

Kneeling in front of the door, I checked the lock. In my time exploring places like Wilten Crags, I had gained some basic lock-picking skills. I dug through my bag and pulled out an amateur kit I had put together myself. It included some wires and some straight, flat tools. Nothing fancy, but it worked in a pinch.

"Here, can you hold this on the door so I can see what I'm doing?" I handed Deckard a light.

With my ear by the door, I worked the wire inside. The pins clicked as I twisted it and moved them up. After a minute or so we were in, and I felt proud of my skills.

In a split second we whisked ourselves inside and closed the door. It wasn't as warm as I had wanted, but any reprieve from the cold was welcome. I rubbed my hands together while I looked around. Hopping over the counter, we headed towards the back where the mail was.

"I'm a little concerned with how easily you did that," Deckard teased me.

"Just something I picked up the last couple years."

I flipped on the lights in the back and began perusing their supplies. We couldn't simply mail ourselves to the city because we'd be caught if we were actually delivered. We were going to have to do something more tricky.

"How about this … Maybe we can mail ourselves somewhere way far away, and then change the address mid-route so we'll end up in storage overnight?"

"Is there even a box here big enough to do that?"

I glanced around. There wasn't even a box big enough for one person, let alone two. It wasn't a great plan anyway. I had no way of knowing if we would have an opportunity to switch the address on it.

"Okay, we can still get it to go where we want if we just make a bunch of packages that need to go that way. We just need to find a way to sneak aboard."

"How?"

"I don't know!" I answered, exasperated. I was doing my best to come up with something. "Maybe we should just go look at the trucks and see if we can figure something out."

We peeked out the back door. Two mail trucks were parked on one side. Another one seemed to be broken down on the other side. It was truly a little postal office.

The back of the trucks had giant doors that opened one way. I motioned for Deckard to follow me as I went to examine one, fiddling with the door to get it open. The inside had racks that went almost all the way to the other end. There was some extra space in the front. Altogether, I estimated it was around thirty feet.

"All right, there's just these two, so if we mess with one, we can make sure they take the one we want," I said.

"That still doesn't take care of how we'll hide, or how we'll make sure they deliver the packages we want them to, first."

"We can just slap stuff on the packages that say they're urgent. And ..." I mulled over the puzzle in my mind. How would we sit in this truck without anyone seeing us?

"Let's check the front seat," Deckard suggested, and I was relieved that he had an idea.

We went to the driver side door and got it open. The front seat stretched from one side to the other. About three people could probably squeeze in, but there was no way a Rhodaren would offer to give us a lift. Deckard nudged me aside and leaned into the truck, moving his hand around the base of the seat.

"What are you looking for?"

"The military trucks we use have a hollow spot under the seats a lot of times. Where you can tuck stuff away. It doesn't look like this opens, though."

"It was a good thought, anyway," I answered.

I wrapped my arms around myself tightly, shivering. Deckard was getting jittery in the cold as well. We needed to figure something out soon.

My eyes wandered all over, searching for inspiration. A chain link fence surrounded the area with a locked gate. The third truck had a flat tire and some bends in the side. It was parked diagonally with the door hanging open – possibly unable to close because of the dents.

"What if we build a false wall?" The words slipped out of my mouth before I'd entirely thought them through.

"What?"

My mind started running. I jogged over to the third truck and grabbed the door.

"We can take this door off..." I checked the back side of it. The outside was painted brown like the rest of the truck, but the inside was a metallic gray. "Look, the back side is the same color as the inside of the truck. If we take this door off, we can make a false wall inside of one of the other trucks and hide behind it."

"You think that'll work?"

"I have no idea! But we won't know until we try. Come on." I waved him over as I pulled on the door. Just as he walked over to me, I rushed back towards the office. "Let's see what kind of tools they have lying around!"

We rummaged through the post office picking up tools and tape. The next hour was spent figuring out how to take the door off. We tried cutting first, then moved on to using wrenches and screwdrivers to take it off the hinges. We took turns pulling on it until it was loose. Once it was off, we carried it inside to remove the hinges completely.

While Deckard finished preparing the door, I grabbed some scraps of paper and sneaked back out to find some addresses to use. The entire time I was writing them down, I bounced in place, unable to stay still. Running back the second I scribbled the last note, I grabbed boxes and put together package after package. I stuck anything I could in them. Rocks from outside, staplers, branches ... anything that would do as filler.

During my search, I happened upon a v-phone. But it didn't seem to have any video, so I guess it was just a phone, phone. After examining the ancient relic for a few seconds, I slipped it into my pocket. It could come in handy later.

I copied their mailing slips until I had an impressive pile and slapped some of their urgent stickers onto some of them. Once I filed them with the other packages, I rejoined Deckard. He just managed to pry the last hinge off when I walked up to him. I grabbed the hinges and stuck them in another package. Might as well get rid of the evidence.

After we carried the door back outside, I left it up to Deckard to sabotage one of the trucks.

"Don't do anything major. I don't want to put anyone in danger," I told him.

"Sure, no problem," he answered confidently.

He came back after a few minutes and helped me carry the door inside the only truck left running. We took it to the back and he held it up from behind.

"Put it back more. It looks weird pushed out that far."

"How about here?" he asked.

I moved around to look at it from different angles. "That looks okay. Any closer and it's too noticeable. How much room do you have?"

"About twenty inches? It's going to be cramped back here. Hey, hold it up."

I set my hands on it to prop it up. "Why?"

55

"I'm going to mark off where it is."

The sound of tape being torn echoed through the truck. As soon as he was done, I slipped behind the door to join him. We spent a long time going through piles of tape to hold it up. By the time we finished every edge was covered in multiple layers. It took almost the entire night to get everything ready, and I was worn out and freezing when it was done. The truck did little to keep the cold out.

I sat on one side with my knees bent and Deckard sat opposite me. Along with only about twenty inches to squeeze in, we also only had about seven feet of space lengthwise. If either of us was alone, it would be enough space to lie down, but split between us both, we had no space to stretch out. And this didn't even take our supplies into account.

"I guess we're not going to get any rest," I lamented. I was curled up because of the cold almost as much as because of the lack of space.

"Forget that," he brushed me off. "Come on, we can lie down."

He stretched out, his feet shoving up against me as he lay down. I squeezed more and more onto my side, squatting on my knees.

"Where am I supposed to go?" I objected.

"Lie on top of me. It's cold anyway, right?"

I paused. Snuggling up to my dad was one thing, but Deckard and I, all things considered, hadn't known each other long. Besides Dad, I'd only slept with Valli, and I knew him for a while before that. Getting that close to someone so soon felt awkward.

"Is that okay?" I hesitated.

"Sure, why not?"

His flippant attitude about it made me wonder if I was being too finicky. It *was* cold and we did need to warm up. It wasn't the time to nitpick. I climbed on top of him and hesitantly settled down, resting my head at his collarbone. He was definitely the warmest thing in the truck. It felt good even if it was awkward. The warmth overwhelmed whatever anxiety I had. His arms came up around my back.

"Sorry. Am I squishing you?" I mumbled.

"Nah, you're not that heavy," he said.

I got as comfortable as I could and drifted off.

Drifting in and out of sleep during the ride, I was vaguely conscious of the truck moving. The longer we stayed in place the more uncomfortable it got. We shifted around to stretch our limbs and wake sleeping body parts. No position could be described as cozy in the cramped space, but we made do.

Deckard kept time to make sure that we didn't pop out in the middle of the day. When the truck stopped moving and we were sure it was evening, we began cutting the tape to free ourselves.

We crawled through the truck to the back door. When we climbed out, the night sky greeted us. There was one major difference from the previous town – this one was covered in a layer of fine snow. The cold bit at me even more than before. How did the Rhodarens stand this weather?

"Okay," my teeth chattered as I spoke, "let's check what town we're in first, then we have to see what information we can find."

We didn't bother breaking into the post office this time. Instead we climbed over the fence and followed the rails to the nearest access panel. I flipped through it. This was where we had been heading.

Good. Now what? The Rhodarens didn't have an organized information system like we did. How they did research was beyond me. It was so readily available to everyone in Nagdecht.

Deckard grabbed my arm while I was thinking and yanked me into the dark corner of a building. A group of Rhodarens walked by. Four of them, strolling along in jackets and coats. Two had fur and leather hats wrapped around their heads. One had her hands in her pockets.

They looked big. Not taller than the average Naggian, but they looked as if they weighed twice as much as I did. Every part of their bodies was bulky, just like the pictures depicted them. I had never seen anyone built like them before. It was strange.

I couldn't tell much else about them in the darkness. They passed by without noticing us.

"They're huge," I whispered to Deckard.

"Yeah, they do make 'em pretty big," he agreed. Deckard was a bit bigger than I was, but nowhere near their size.

Hidden by the shadows, I sat down. I envied them and their coats. They strolled around like they were plenty warm. Deckard squatted next to me, resting his chin in the palm of his hand.

"How are we going to find out where this person lives? I couldn't find any information on people. Just businesses and stuff," I muttered, irritated.

"I don't know. Call someone?"

His suggestion gave me pause. On the surface, it sounded ridiculous, but it could work. Without video, we could talk to someone without being caught. No one would ever suspect we were from another country.

"You could be onto something. We just need someplace to call, and maybe we could pretend to be lost travelers or something."

"We need a phone, too," he reminded me.

I pulled the tiny phone out of my pocket. "I have one."

He blinked in surprise. "Where did you get that?"

"I found it back at the post office. Still," I rubbed my arms with extra enthusiasm to emphasize my point, "can't we find somewhere warm?"

We stumbled to our feet. My legs already felt numb. Breaking into a small business would probably be easy, but we needed to find a place we could call first. Which meant finding someplace where people were still awake.

We wandered around until we found a street that still had businesses with their lights on. The outside identified one as a bar, one as a lounge, and one of the others as some sort of club.

"Of course it would be a bar. Galloughs always keeps the bar open late," I whispered to myself.

Deckard glanced at me. "You hang out at the bars a lot?" He sounded surprised.

"Not really. I just know someone who runs one," I explained. "Anyway, we have the name of a place and know it's open. Maybe we can figure out how to call it now."

Another trip to the access panel finally produced results. The one thing they had plenty of was addresses, and it took me a bit to figure out, but the strings of numbers listed with them were for the phone. It was an unusual way to call someone, for sure. How would people ever remember a series of random numbers like that for every place? I preferred Nagdecht's system. All I needed was to know who or where someone was, and I could easily call them.

The cold urged me to search faster and I quickly found a nearby business that looked like a sandwich shop, which was all the better for us. We hustled there and broke in. It was tiny, with just a couple of tables. Deckard started making us something to eat while I made use of the phone to call the bar.

A gruff voice answered one the other side, "Checkpoint Bar, what do you need?"

"Hello? I'm visiting the town and was hoping I could ask for some help. I have this address, but I'm not sure how to get there."

"This is a bar. Can't you just call them up and ask for directions?" she asked.

"Sorry, it's actually from some paperwork, I don't have their number. Do you know how I could find them?"

"I've got a lot of work here. I don't have time to look up stuff for you."

"Please, I'm not from around here. If you could just tell me where to go …"

She let out a heavy sigh. "What's the paperwork for?"

"It's an appraiser's. I want to talk to her about the item she has."

"Then I'd suggest looking for the place that appraised it. They'll be the ones who know."

No central information system to get everything from? This was going to be difficult.

"There's no better way?"

"That's all I can tell you. I've gotta go." She hung up.

Before I could anguish over my poor results, a sandwich plopped down on the table in front of me. My gaze flitted up to Deckard before I inspected its contents. I didn't recognize everything in it, but it couldn't be too bad.

"Can we just stay here?" I asked as I took a bite. It had a strange, sweet taste somewhere in the middle. I rolled it over my tongue and tried to identify it. Some sort of sweet pickle?

"I wouldn't mind, but I think the owner would complain," he answered, sitting next to me.

We ate and enjoyed the warmth for a time, reluctant to walk back out into the cold. But we had no choice. If we stayed too long, we could be risking our lives.

I looked up the name of the appraiser's on my documents, and we headed back out. Going there would be our next step. I managed to locate it on their maps, but it was a long walk. My legs were a strange combination of stiff, sore, and numb. I could feel them just enough to make out the stiff and sore part.

The longer we walked, the more I wished we could make use of their rails, but even if we had a Rhodaren ID to use and found an empty cart, there could still be people waiting to board it if we stopped. It was too great a risk.

So instead, we walked. We walked, and we shivered. The cold was even getting to Deckard. The Geuranian military uniform wasn't meant for snowy weather.

We were running out of hours in the night when we finally reached the appraiser's. It was a plain two-story building, like a rectangle with a door and some windows slapped on. It wasn't well protected and breaking in was no big deal. Finding the information we needed proved to be a greater challenge.

We rummaged through cabinets until we found more recent documents. According to them, she didn't have it appraised there but at another branch in another town. It wasn't what I wanted, but at least it gave us a direction.

We went back out to the access panel again to figure out a way. I set down the papers on the panel for reference as I browsed for the best course to take. If she had it appraised at the other location, then she probably lived near it.

While I was studying it, Deckard yanked me away. Snatching at the papers, the tips of my fingers barely grazed them and they fluttered to the ground. I fought with him in order to get them, but his grip was tight and he dragged me away.

A woman walked towards us. She held a cane and moved at a leisurely pace.

We ducked down behind a nearby fence, keeping our eyes on the papers that sat on the thin layer of snow. No matter. They had no meaning to anyone else; we could just get them back once she left.

The woman strolled up to the panel. Her age was noticeable, written all over her face in the form of creases. Her auburn coat was thick, but worn. As she slowed, her eyes turned to the ground. She bent down, picking up the fallen papers and scanning them. I expected her to throw them away or something.

But she didn't. An expression of shock crossed her face as she stared at the papers.

"Thank Pressea," she muttered under her breath, eyes turning to the sky momentarily before she packed the papers into her bag. *No! Those are my papers!*

She went back down the street and I inched out of my hiding spot, watching after her.

"She took our information!" I whispered urgently to Deckard.

"What can we do about it?"

"We need to get it back!" I started running after her before I even thought about it. Deckard darted after me. His hand scraped my back in an attempt to grab me, but I wasn't about to be stopped.

The farther she went, the more dangerous things became. She hobbled to an area of the town that still had lights on, and we were forced to crawl behind things, keeping an eye out for wandering Rhodarens. Watching her slowly leave with our papers was frustrating. I wished I could just reach out and snatch them from her.

We followed her to a bar and were forced to wait outside for her to appear again. Fidgeting

restlessly, we ducked down across the street and watched her through a window.

She went to the counter, borrowing a pen and paper before sitting at a table with a drink. For several agonizing minutes, we couldn't do anything. Then, she stood, walked over to the side of the bar, and posted the paper up on a bulletin board. It was one among several papers pinned up.

When she left the bar our pursuit was cut short; she boarded a cart and there was no way we could follow without major risk of getting caught. I grabbed the side of my head, letting out a frustrated growl. We'd just lost everything we had, and there was nothing we could do about it.

It was then that I realized something. She just posted something inside. It could have her information. I grabbed Deckard and we headed back to the bar, but had to dive to the ground when a truck passed by. We fumbled back to our feet to continue on, but it slowed to a stop in front of the bar. Seeing an individual drive themselves somewhere instead of using a cart was odd.

A man stepped out of the truck. From behind, I could only tell he had a bag slung over his shoulder and curly hair. His long jacket had a tail in the back with a slit in it. Each side hung down to his knees. With his left arm resting on the bag, he walked into the bar.

After he went in, I dared to get closer to the bar, looking for an opportunity to see something useful. The man went over to the board immediately, looking over all the papers posted on it. He spent some time before touching the paper the old woman had posted. He scrutinized it, then snatched the flyer off the wall and headed back to his truck.

While he got in, I grabbed onto the back. Wherever he was going, he'd taken her flyer. I pulled open the doors on the back of the truck and jumped in, Deckard following behind me in a panic.

"What are you doing?" he asked, trying to keep his voice down.

I tried to keep myself steady as I pulled the doors closed, leaving us in the dark. "She took our stuff and he took her flyer. We have to find her and get our stuff back!" Without it, I only had a vague notion of where to go.

Digging through my bag, I found one of my lights and flicked it on. It dimly lit the back of the truck which was empty. At least we wouldn't have to worry about him coming back here to get his things. Hopefully, he wouldn't be loading it with anything anytime soon.

The truck rumbled along for short while, then stopped. We waited in silence. After several minutes, I slowly opened the back door of the truck. It was still dark outside. I slid out as quietly as I could and crawled along the ground until I could see the driver side window. The truck was empty.

We were in front of some sort of little house. It was run down, looking like it needed more than a few repairs. Large patches of paint were missing – I couldn't tell what color in the dark. One of the windows was taped up in a corner, and the wooden fence that partially surrounded it had pieces missing and swayed in the wind. I crawled back to the truck and got in the back, closing the doors again.

"I think we're at the guy's house," I told Deckard.

"Yeah? What now?"

"Sleep?" I suggested. We hadn't gotten a good night of rest before. It had been cold and cramped. It was still cold, but at least the truck was empty and we could use all of the space.

"You think we'll be caught in here?"

"I don't know, but where else are we going to go?" I rubbed my arms. "It's still cold, but at least we have lots of room."

We stretched out, but the cold made it uncomfortable to stay like that. Eventually I curled up next to Deckard, using him for warmth. He made a light quip about being my 'personal heater,' but he wanted the extra heat as much as I did.

When I woke up, my back was cold, but my front was relatively warm. My hands, legs, and forehead were pressed against Deckard. I twisted my stiff shoulders and rolled over. It took a moment to realize that we were moving. I sat up and moved to the doors, waiting to see what was going on.

9

5, 7, 3399
Firsday

She walked from the bedroom to the living room with the picture in her shaking hand. The young woman and man in the photograph hugged each other with smiles on their faces. Her hand trembled.

She laid it flat on the table. Her chest felt tight. The fingers of her other hand strangled the handle of a knife, clenching until her knuckles lightened from the pressure. Then she drew it up. With several wide strokes she stabbed it, pressing the knife harder into the picture each time.

While she was swinging, the door opened. The knife stood in place on its own, piercing the table through the picture as she glared down at it. A man stood in the doorway, his hand on the frame. He had thick, wavy hair and a small crook in his nose. A bag slung over his shoulder hung at his hip with the head of a lympet poking out of the front. His hand rested comfortably on the bag just behind her large, round ears that came to a soft point.

The woman's eyes turned to him as he surveyed the scene. Her leaning over the table. The knife sticking out of it. A cold, bitter glare aimed his way.

"Were you the one looking for help?" he broke the silence.

Her fingers dug at the table.

He didn't wait long to continue. "My name is Delmar. You're Breigah, right? I have my own truck. If you can make good on your end of the deal I'll take you wherever you want."

"Get. Out," her words came out low and threatening.

He lifted his eyebrows, hesitating before he scooted out of the doorway to the front yard. His eyes turned to the lympet in the bag. "Did we get the wrong person?"

He waited until he heard a thumping behind him. She stood in the doorway with cane in hand. Her demeanor had calmed. For a moment she was silent.

"This is your truck?" she asked.

He slapped the hood. "That's right. And you? You're the one offering the deed, right, Granny?"

"That's me. I have a map right here." She rummaged through her bag, pulling out some paperwork and handing it to him. He skimmed it over, looking at the directions.

"A bit vague, but I should be able to do it. This is a tiny town, a decent drive away," he said. "When will you be ready to go?"

"I'm ready to go right now," she answered, hobbling towards the passenger door. Though she carried the cane, she didn't lean heavily on it. He watched her, a hint of unease in the pit of his stomach.

"Need some help up, Granny?"

"I can get in fine. I'm not that old yet," she declined as she climbed into the truck.

His eyes wandered back to the home. It was a quaint house – not terrible by any means. Small with a rustic feel. A good wooden floor and interior that gave it a warm feeling. And yet something was off about it. Even more than the fact that he had just watched her stab a table.

He pulled his gaze away and got into the truck, resting his bag on the seat next to him.

The woman sat with both hands on the head of her cane. "Aren't you a little old for a lympet?"

He grinned. "I'll have you know she's my one and only."

With a glance she inspected the bag, before looking ahead and nodding towards the windshield.

One hand on the steering wheel and one hanging over the back of the seat, he turned the truck around and began driving.

"It's going to be a long drive. Bathroom breaks every two hours," he told her. She didn't respond.

The silence was overwhelming. Then he flipped on the radio. Music belted out loudly and he relaxed.

Hours later, he pulled to a stop in front of a small appraisal shop. Hopping out, he moved around to help her. She accepted his hand as she climbed down to the ground.

"There should be a bathroom in there if you need it." He pointed out the nearby building. "I recommend going now and getting anything you need. I'll check out this place." He jogged into the appraiser's while she wandered into a nearby store.

The office was manned by one woman at a counter. She glanced up, asking with some forced cheer, "May I help you?"

"Actually, I have some questions about a client you saw …"

Her eyes dropped to the bag at his side. A fuzzy face poked out, and her smile turned from forced to genuine. "Aww, she's so cute."

Lifting his bag up onto the counter, he smirked. "She always gets all the attention," he joked lightly. The lympet twitched an ear. Running her fingers through the dirty white fur, she leaned on the counter.

"So you remember her? It's a small town, right? Do you know her?" he asked.

"She doesn't live here. I can't give out confidential information like her address, but I did notice her around town."

71

"Really? Was she up to something?"

"Maybe just getting some food and such. She did stop by the 'Top Advantage' store. I don't know anything besides that."

"Well, you've been a big help." He shot her a glowing smile. "Thank you very much."

With that, he jogged out of the building with his furry partner. It was a short walk to the convenience store. Being one of the larger shops in the town, it had three employees on duty at once. An amused huff escaped him. Quaint towns had a charm to them.

After some questioning of a young man behind the counter, he discovered that the clerk remembered the woman coming in and purchasing a large first aid kit. He also knew that the woman lived out of town, down the mountain.

He headed back to the edge of town where the old woman was coming back to the truck. He picked up his pace to join her.

"Hey, Granny. I've got some info. That woman doesn't live in town. If we take the road east, down the mountain, we'll eventually come to her place. She's some sort of botanist who lives out in the boonies."

"All right." She nodded. "Shall we go, then?"

"Not quite yet. Feenie needs a chance to make a pit stop," he explained, tilting his head down towards his bag. "We'll be back in just a minute."

She continued hobbling towards the truck without him. When she rounded the front of the truck she was in for the shock of her life.

Had she met with a thief she would have been surprised, but this was far beyond that. She had to pause to decide if she wasn't hallucinating. There, by the passenger side door, was a Nadder holding her bag. He looked up at her with wide eyes. For a brief moment that felt all too long they stared at each other in stunned silence.

The Nadder fleeing prompted her to finally react. She screamed.

From his spot behind a building Delmar rushed around the corner to see what happened. When he heard her shout, "thief," it became clear. He scooped up the lympet that was still sniffing at the ground and darted towards the truck.

He, too, saw a sight that shocked him. A Nadder was across the street with the old woman's bag, but more than that, there was a Geuranian in full military uniform, too. And they were hijacking a snowmobile.

"Hey!"

Their eyes turned towards him, but it only seemed to inspire them to flee even more.

He jogged back to the truck. Her bag was missing from the front seat. Grabbing her arm, he nearly tossed her in before running around to jump into the driver's seat. He started it and spun around to give chase. The snowmobile was well ahead with the Nadder holding onto the Geuranian as they sped away.

"You're seeing what I'm seeing, right?" he asked her, considering the possibility that he was hallucinating. "Is that a Nadder and a Geuranian?"

"It looks like." The strange occurrence even gave her pause as she stared ahead. The absence of her bag quickly rankled her when she unconsciously grabbed for it, only to feel air. "What about my bag? Without that, there's no deal," her voice was soft but firm.

"Don't worry, we'll get it back. They're heading for the mountain pass to the east," he assured her.

He placed both hands on the wheel, keeping a steady pace through the snow. The snowmobile pulled farther and farther ahead. When they began making rounds down the mountain they nearly lost sight of the pair on the snowmobile.

"They're going to get away," her voice tensed.

"Don't worry. A Geuranian isn't going to outdrive me in the snow. And he's driving stupid," he answered, keeping steady and focused on the road. A weak, wooden fence covered small portions of the turns. It nearly made him laugh. What a waste of effort. The fence was too weak to stop even a snowmobile and whoever built it had only bothered to place it in a few of the many treacherous spots.

He knew what was coming when he saw the sharp turn up ahead. The snowmobile attempted to slow for the turn. The Geuranian struggled with it, slamming on the breaks repeatedly as it flew over the icy path. When he turned the handle, the snowmobile toppled over sideways. The Nadder tumbled off from behind while the Geuranian propelled towards the edge with the vehicle. He rammed through a wooden fence with it, easily breaking through and disappearing down the mountainside. The Nadder clawed futilely at the ground until he, too, vanished from sight over the edge.

Breigah gasped. Delmar parked the truck on the corner of the path. Stepping out, he approached the fence. The side of the mountain was steep and evergreen trees covered it and its base. Below him, the Nadder clung to rock and vine.

Delmar leaned on the fence, his weight testing the limits of the creaky old wood. "What's wrong? Don't know how to drive in snow?"

The Nadder struggled to find something to grab. His feet scraped the rocks. Delmar kicked a pile of snow over the edge. The Nadder winced as the dirt and snow hit his face, shaking it away from his head. "Stop that!"

"Just get my bag." The woman approached from behind.

"Can I borrow that, Granny?" He reached out a hand for her cane. She tossed it to him, staying steady on her feet. He lifted a brow. "Nice toss."

Holding the shaft, he maneuvered the handle to grab the strap of the bag. The Nadder wiggled around on the side, trying to ward it off. It was no use. He had nowhere to go.

"What kind of men steal from grannies?" he scolded the Nadder as he lifted the bag away.

"She took it from us! Those are our documents," he snapped back, his arms shaking.

"Ours now." He glanced back, holding the cane out for the woman.

The Nadder's grip gave away and he gasped. He tumbled down the cliff with nothing to grab and nothing to stop him. Delmar watched him until he disappeared below the trees.

He leaned over the fence, mumbling to the woman, "I wonder if he's still alive," before he raised his voice, shouting, "Are you still alive down there?"

There was a pause before he heard a response from below, "I hate you so much."

His eyes turned to the woman as he stated matter-of-factly, "He's still alive." Opening the bag, he pulled out the paperwork and flipped through it. "It's all still here." A piece of information grabbed his eye. "Hey, this says this thing came from Nagdecht ..." He paused uncomfortably. "I guess that explains the Nadder."

Walking back to the truck, he wasted no time turning the radio back on. Music gave him the cover he needed to consider what he saw. As they pulled away, a song started up, a slow, sad waltz. After it played for a few seconds the woman began shaking. She stared away from him out the window.

At first, he ignored her. He didn't want to pry and she didn't want him to pry. But after a minute she held her head in her hands and began sobbing. He found himself leaning away with his arm resting on the window frame. The chill mountain air was a more desirable companion than the woman next to him.

"Awkward ..." he muttered under his breath, glancing down at Feenie.

The strange woman, a Nadder, and a Geuranian. He couldn't help but feel that something was off about the entire situation.

10
5, 7, 3399
Firsday

The truck pulled to a stop. I pressed an ear against the wall, hearing a short conversation between a man and woman.

It was hours later before the truck stopped again. Silence took up residence for a while before I cautiously cracked the door of the truck open. No one was across the street. It looked like the edge of a town. Some small snowmobiles were parked across the way. There was a building and then the road seemed to descend down some sort of mountainside.

Snow greeted my feet when I hopped down. I peeked around the end of the truck.

"I think it's clear," I whispered to Deckard. I crept along the side of the truck to the passenger door. There, on the front seat, sat a familiar bag. I ducked lower when I heard some voices, but they were still on the other side of the truck. They mentioned a road going east, but the bag was just within my reach.

I slipped my hand through the door and snatched it, but just as I did, the old woman came around the front side of the truck. We both froze in place. I was absolutely terrified. If she attracted attention, I could get beaten down by a mob.

After staring for all too long, I finally came to my senses and ran for it. Then she screamed.

"Where are we going?" Deckard hopped out of the truck to run with me as soon as I blazed by.

"I don't know. Let's just get out of here before anyone sees us!" I said. We rushed over to one of the snowmobiles.

"Come on!" I urged Deckard, waiting for him to get on first.

"I don't know how to drive one of these." Deckard cocked a brow at me.

"Well, I don't know how to drive anything, so you're probably the better choice," I retorted.

He climbed onto the front and played with the handles. Tilting his head, he scanned over the few controls. I threw the bag over my shoulder and hopped on behind him.

"Hurry!" I nudged him.

He grumbled back, "Give me a minute. I don't know how this thing works."

"Hey!"

A voice from across the road jolted me upright. The Rhodaren who had been driving had popped back out from behind the building.

"Come on!" I tugged on Deckard. The snowmobile bolted forward. I flopped backwards before digging my fingers into him and clinging to his back.

"Sorry."

"Just go! Go!" My arms trembled because of the near fall, but I held on. The man ran towards us, but redirected himself as we pulled away. We moved more smoothly as Deckard gained control.

"Outside of the town, no one should be there," I yelled in his ear. He steered us towards the mountain path. Balancing on the vehicle felt strange, and I found myself holding onto Deckard so tightly that I could break his ribs. If I didn't, I thought I would topple over at the slightest turn.

The truck soon rumbled behind us. Each time I looked back, it seemed to be farther away. I breathed a sigh of relief. I pressed my face against Deckard's back and held onto my stomach the best I could as we went down the treacherous slopes. Every bump incited a fresh wave of adrenaline. How sore was I going to be when we parked?

Then the snowmobile skidded. I could feel Deckard hitting the breaks, but it wasn't stopping. There was a turn up ahead and we were going too fast to make it.

"Deckard, the edge!" I yelled.

"I know!" he snapped back, struggling with the bike. He attempted to turn despite the speed, but his unstable movements caused it to teeter. It slid and crashed over on its side. I was thrown back, gliding along as if I was going down a slide covered in wax. He flew across the ice ahead of me, still on the bike.

The snowmobile crashed through a wooden fence and plunged off the edge. Deckard followed shortly after. I had no time to spare a thought for him as I grabbed desperately at the ground. Even though I slowed, it wasn't enough to make a difference. I slipped underneath a fence and straight off the ledge. Clawing at the cliff, I managed to grab something. My hands stung from the cuts and scrapes, but I stopped.

For several moments, I hung there. Gazing down, the mountainside was steep. My eyes scanned the area for anything I could use to climb, but everything was covered in a sheet of snow. Even if there were more crevices, they might have been filled in with it. There weren't many vines or branches sticking out. I had knocked the snow off the ones I had in my hands, creating a trail down the side of the mountain where I had polished it.

When I looked up, the Rhodaren man was leering over the side.

"What's wrong? Don't know how to drive in snow?" the man asked, teasing.

I gave him as hard a glare as I could, but keeping myself from falling took precedent. No matter where I reached, there was nothing solid to grab. He scraped his foot along the ground and threw some snow over the edge. Some cold specks hit my face. I winced and shook them off. "Stop that!"

"Just get the map," I barely heard a woman say. I couldn't see her from where I was. The man looked behind himself and reached for something.

"Can I borrow that, Granny?" and then, "Nice toss."

A second later, he reached over the edge with a cane, prodding my side with the handle. "What kind of men steal from grannies?"

My face heated up with anger. "She took it from us! Those are our documents!"

"Ours now," he responded cheerfully.

My limbs trembled. I couldn't hook my foot onto anything and my arms and fingers ached. Time crawled by as my grip deteriorated. Finally, I slipped. Everything flew by in a blur as I rolled down the steep cliff at lightning speeds. I was fortunate that there wasn't much to hit on the way down. It also meant there was nothing to stop me.

I rolled all the way to the bottom. I tucked into a ball as the ground curved from a steep angle to flat land. Even when I slowed and stopped, I wasn't sure if it was over because my head was still spinning. Flat on the ground, my first attempts at movement failed and I ate snow. All around me were trees with spiky needles and bushes covered in a layer of frost. I lay in a sickening daze.

"Are you still alive down there?" a voice echoed from above.

My mind was in a haze. It took a minute for the question's meaning to register. I wrapped an arm around my stomach, glaring at the sky above before screaming as loud as I could, "I hate you so much!"

The world slowly stopped spinning and settled on being wobbly and uncooperative. I fumbled to my feet and hobbled about. One thought swept through my mind.

"Deckard!" I called for him, waiting for an answer. *He fell down here somewhere.* I stumbled around, slapping away branches and searching for him.

Then I saw his legs sticking out from some brush. I jogged over, stumbling on the way. He wasn't moving. His body had crushed a few small bushes and he was lying still on top of it. I didn't see the snowmobile anywhere – no doubt it was in pieces somewhere.

"Deckard!" I screamed. *No! This can't be happening!*

My thoughts were a muddy mess as I knelt by him and tried to come up with some idea of what to do. I held my hands up, almost afraid to touch him and do something wrong, before placing my ear on his chest. His heart beat softly and steadily.

A trickle of relief flowed through me before the panic flooded back up. He wasn't getting up. Why wasn't he getting up? I didn't see any blood beyond a few small cuts, nor did anything look broken to my untrained eyes. I placed my hand above his nose and mouth but I didn't feel any warm air.

My eyes widened with fear. I moved my hand closer - still nothing. I didn't know what to do. Taking a deep breath, I bent over him.

Suddenly one of his eyes snapped open. I jumped back, unable to even form a word. "Ah ...?"

A grinned formed on his lips. He pushed himself up with an elbow. "I couldn't hold my breath any longer."

"You ...!" It took a moment to come up with the words. "You jerk!"

I struggled to my feet, slapping away the needles and snow as I stomped away.

"You don't need to get so upset." He rolled to his side with a small laugh, then groaned. "I could use a little help here."

"Get up yourself!" I kept my back to him.

"Come on, it was just a joke." He floundered around until he finally managed get his feet under him.

"You'll be lucky if I help you next time!" I yelled back at him, marching on.

"I'm lucky I wasn't hurt this time. With how long you were taking I'd have been dead."

Deckard didn't understand how badly he'd scared me. He had gone too far. I was terrified, and I felt embarrassed that it was all a ruse.

We walked in silence for a long time. He fell behind me as I charged ahead without waiting. It was Deckard who first dared to break the silence.

"… So, are you still mad at me?"

"Yes!" I snapped.

He waited only a second. "How about now?"

"Yes," I answered again irritation obvious in my voice.

He waited another second. "How about now?"

I rolled my eyes and looked at him. At first glance, he had an unrepentant grin on his face, but I saw a twinge of worry in his eyes. I sighed, controlling my aggravation as much as possible. "No."

He trotted up to join me. My glare was harsh when it settled on him. I marched on with my arms clamped around myself. I was cold. I was bruised. I was mad. Everything was going wrong and I couldn't seem to fix any of it. The Rhodarens had our information and we were in some sort of weird looking forest.

"Forest" was being generous. Trees sparsely decorated the landscape. They went as far as the eye could see, but there was tons of space between them. A white blanket covered everything.

A grimace was glued to my face and I kept my ears folded down. The tips were going to freeze off if I didn't figure out something soon.

"Where are you going?"

"I'm heading east," I answered curtly.

"That's going to be a long walk," he muttered.

"It's going to take longer if we stand still."

Our conversation died. My anger wouldn't let me talk to him for long. Hours passed. We trudged along. After a time, my mind began wandering away from him. Was the weather going to kill us if we stayed out here? The longer we went, the more beat down I felt. Snow began coming down and the cold specks hit and stung my face. We couldn't sleep outside like this. It wasn't like Nagdecht or Geuran. Chances were high that we could freeze to death.

Somehow I pushed on, staring at the ground.

"Deckard," I spoke up weakly. His eyes turned toward me. "We've got to do something. We're going to freeze out here."

He didn't answer, but I didn't get the sense he was ignoring me. His eyes flitted around to the snow and trees, concern in them. I suspected he was trying to think of an idea, but was coming up short.

"Do you think we can make a fire?" I asked. My body rejected the idea of rubbing sticks together. It was already aching and tired, but it was no use. We had to do something.

"Y ..." he hesitated, his voice sounding unsure, "Yeah, I think we could. I've got some matches."

"You think it'll stay lit in this weather?" I was doubtful.

"Sure, if we got it going good," he gained confidence as he talked.

We began gathering wood and digging a hole, building a makeshift fire pit. When we had a pile built up, Deckard lit a match. Protecting it from the wind with his hand, he held it to the wood. I watched in anticipation. For too long the flames didn't care for our wood pile. Worried that we would waste our matches, I grabbed a clump of old pine needles from the ground and shook off the snow.

The flame engulfed them in a split second, and we scampered around to gather more to keep it going until it took to the pile of wood. Seeing it light up barely eased my fears. We had no tent and hardly anything to use to keep ourselves warm. I scooted close to the flames, our only source of heat.

Deckard grabbed my shoulder and pulled me away.

"Hey!" I wrinkled my nose at him.

"Don't sit downwind of it," he warned me.

"Oh," my tone softened.

We both sat upwind of the fire. I held my hands over it. Every time I pulled away, I quickly missed the warmth.

After a long day, I found myself staring blankly at the fire. Exhausted. Mulling things over, and feeling awkward with Deckard. I didn't want things to be this way. Darkness was creeping up on us. Snow was everywhere, and we were surrounded by the weird looking trees. Black silhouettes lingered all around us. Towering, sharp, and dead.

"Something wrong?" Deckard asked while I scanned the area.

"Everything here wants to stab us," I replied with my ears lowered.

"Huh?"

"Look at those trees. It's like every branch ends in a sharp point. And the leaves ..." I picked up one of the needles. "They're all thin and pointed." I pushed the tip of the needle against his bare skin. The needle flexed as I put pressure on it. I stabbed at him a few times to make my point.

He brushed the needle away. "It's fine. They're just trees, and we're out here by ourselves."

Black night, white snow. Whatever life this forest had was hiding well. I only ever caught any movement from the corner of my eye, and every time I wondered if I really saw anything. I missed the colorful environment back home. Flowers and trees and fruits in every shade imaginable. Everything looked so dreary here. The longer we sat out in the cold, the more it felt like this country was covered in a blanket of death. Rhodarens must have invested everything they had in good heaters.

"Deckard ..." I murmured.

"Yeah?"

"I'm scared."

I wondered if he was going to tease me, but he stayed quiet, sitting with one leg bent in front of him and the other tucked under it with his arm hanging over his knee. His eyes flicked around. Surely he saw unwelcoming silhouettes and black sky as well. Maybe he didn't know what to say.

"Do you think we're going to be okay?" I asked.

"Sure, we'll be fine," his cheery voice wavered. He reached over to our bags. "We've got some stuff. One of us can get all wrapped up. If we stay close together, it'll help. And we can take turns watching the fire."

He pulled out the extra clothing we had and started wrapping it around me. I only had one extra jacket in my bag. He had an extra uniform in his. I pulled my jacket around me, and his over it. It provided some relief, blocking out a little bit of the cold. He set down our bags to make himself a pillow.

"Are you okay?" I asked.

"I'm all right. You can go ahead and sleep first," he said.

After our previous experiences, getting close to him wasn't as awkward. I put it out of my mind when I climbed on top of him. We both desperately needed the warmth. I squished one ear against his chest to keep it warm and dragged a loose jacket over the other one. With the fire, the extra cover, and him, I managed to keep mildly warm. I was so tired, I drifted off despite it all.

11
5, 8, 3399
Liddenday

"The sound of explosions whistling through the air, the Rhodarens are coming, the camp is gone, run, run, five-sixteen, the fate of the nation depends on you ..."

I rustled, hearing a quiet murmuring as I slowly gained consciousness.

"... even though your legs ache and your lungs hurt, you're halfway there ..."

It was Deckard mumbling some song to himself. When I opened my eyes again, the horizon was bathed in orange and the sky was a light blue. Deckard was prodding at the waning fire. I sat up. A thin layer of snow fell off of me. He stopped singing as I moved.

Deckard looked tired, but he put on a smile. "Finally up?"

I took in my surroundings. It wasn't dark at all anymore. "You stayed up all night."

"Eh," he shrugged, "I couldn't get to sleep anyway."

His eyes looked heavy, and he was even paler than normal. I wasn't sure if I was imagining it, but there was a blue tint to the tips of his ears.

"Are you going to be okay? You look like you're freezing, and we still have a long way to go."

He ran a hand over his clothes, brushing them off. "I'm all right."

For a moment, I hesitated to give up my extra clothing. The idea of the cold hitting me again left me reluctant, but I couldn't leave Deckard like that. I pulled his jacket off and wrapped it around him. My fingers dug into my extra jacket and I braced myself for the incoming shock as I pulled it off to cover up Deckard more.

He gently held it against himself. I wasn't positive what to do, but we couldn't sit there. I covered the fire with snow, then helped Deckard stand up. We had to keep moving east. At the very least, we had been carried much of the way in the back of that truck, but our destination was still far. I doubted Deckard's ability to walk the whole way, not to mention my own.

"I'll figure out a way for us to get a ride, don't worry," I assured him. He needed rest and somewhere warm to stay.

I stayed close to him. His weight on my shoulder increased as we walked. The more time dragged on, the more I thought that I wouldn't be able to keep my promise to him. There didn't seem to be anything beyond trees and endless sheets of white. Fear nagged at me.

Then we came upon what seemed to be the road. More importantly, it was the road that led from the mountain path. It would keep us going the right way, at least. We stumbled along the path until we crossed a shed. I didn't see any signs of life. Just a shed, an outhouse, and some old, abandoned tools. It looked like an abandoned pit stop. Tire tracks were embedded in the snow, going down, down, down, so someone had been around recently.

I could think of at least two someones who were going this way. Maybe we were getting close.

With his arm over my shoulder, I walked Deckard into the shed to sit down for a bit. If nothing else, it would get us out of the snow, and it gave me a break to figure out how to travel east.

There wasn't much in the shed. An old table and some tools stacked in a corner. I didn't get the impression they had been used in the last decade.

It still didn't add up to anything, but at least Deckard was getting a break. He sat with his back to the wall and had his arms wrapped around himself. Sleep was stalking him but not quite taking over. His obvious exhaustion made me cringe. This was an emergency.

I tossed my bag on the table. It slid off and hit the ground. With a drawn out sigh, I went to pick it up, placing a hand on the table. The surface was deceptively smooth, and it felt sturdy. Sliding down the mountainside, we had barely been able to slow ourselves.

I grabbed the legs of the table and lifted it up. It was an oval shape with legs that curved and ended in little balls at the end.

"Deckard, I think I figured out a way to travel faster."

"Nn?" He glanced up wearily.

"We can use this." I held the table up.

"How can we use that?"

"We can slide it on the snow. We're heading down."

"How will we steer it?"

"I don't know. I guess we'd just have to use our weight or sticks or something. It's worth a try, at least!" I rushed outside alone, letting him rest.

Outside I placed the table upside-down on the snow and tested how well it slid. It inched down the hill when I let go of it. I grabbed the leg and held it.

"Deckard!" I called for him. He shuffled out of the shed. "It looks like it might work!"

I hoped the incline was enough to get us moving. Deckard took a seat first while I held it still.

"Ready?"

He glanced back at me doubtfully. "As ready as I'll ever be." I felt the same as him.

"Here goes nothing!" I grabbed the two back legs and sprinted forward. The table flew over the snow. When it began going too fast for me to keep up with it, I hopped on and plopped down. At first it slowed under my weight. For a while, I thought it would stop, but bit by bit it sped up. The ground beneath the snow was like a layer of ice and gave little friction.

Then it went too fast. I clung onto a leg and Deckard. Fear about our lack of steering welled up. We struggled to shift the direction it went by leaning one way. Our control was poor at best.

Soon the wind was slapping us in the face. Using Deckard as a windbreaker, I could barely see anything. Thoughts of trying to control the table were long gone. All I could think of was holding on for dear life. My heart raced. I lost track of time. We were whipped to the side when it slid along a curve. Holding on became a painful test of strength and endurance. Icy wind stung my face. Everything whizzed by so fast.

Somehow we managed to cling on. We only stopped when we plowed through a pile of snow. Snow rained over us and, for a moment, the world was nothing but white.

When I wobbled to my feet I had to look down to make sure I was all still there. Deckard staggered in front of me. I couldn't tell if it was exhaustion or the ride that left him barely able to stand. Possibly both. Clapping sounds filled the air as he brushed off.

I glanced behind us. How far had we gone? Without knowing how fast we were going or for how long, it was impossible to tell. My body felt like it had been tense for an hour. We'd probably done over a day's worth of traveling in a flash.

After that, we walked with renewed vigor in our steps. Our veins had more adrenaline in them than blood. I checked the map in my head, but I couldn't determine how far we were from the greenhouse. We had to keep going and hope for the best.

When a building finally came into view, it was a relief. It was a huge place with a roof high enough to accommodate a second or third floor. We hesitated to approach. No one else seemed to be out here for miles and miles. If someone was there, they were probably alone. The truck wasn't anywhere in sight, and the snow had covered any tracks it would have left.

It wasn't a solitary building. There were sheds and tiny shack-like structures that all looked to serve some sort of purpose. I guessed to house tools and maybe some living conveniences. There was also a large lake, but it was frozen over.

With it down to us and a building, we glanced at each other.

"There's no town or anything here. It's just this building in the middle of nowhere ..." I said. He looked so worn down, it pained me. Before he had taken the cold better than I had, but now I could swear he was shivering worse than I was.

The trembling affected his voice, making him speak unevenly. "Well, this is the place, isn't it?" I had to do something. I was really worried about him.

"It should be. It's supposed to be a place where they grow plants, so I thought it would have glass walls or something. But it looks like it's built solid."

"It's pretty big." He pointed at the roof briefly, but his arm instantly returned to hug his torso. "The roof looks like it's glass."

There was a dome structure that amazingly didn't have much snow on it. It was entirely see-through.

93

"I guess that would be to let in the sun. What should we do? Try to go in?"

"Someone's gotta be around here."

I nodded. Whoever registered the statue wrote this down as their address. A strange place to stay.

"Whoever it is, it looks like they're probably alone. I wonder if it's safe to talk to them. Do you think they can make phone calls from out here?"

"No idea. If they called someone up and said a Geuranian and a Na -- Naggian were outside they would probably think they're crazy." He let out an amused huff. A puff of white vapor drifted through the air when he did.

I stared at the door. His condition gave me a new sense of urgency. The building could have a solution to our problem, if it was warm inside.

"Let's go for it," I said with an amount of confidence that surprised even me.

I stomped up to the door and knocked on it. When nothing happened, I pounded louder.

It cracked open slightly and I glimpsed the woman on the other side before her eyes widened and she slammed it. I barely caught my foot in the door before it closed.

"Ow!" I cried, pleading with her, "Wait! We're not here to hurt anyone! We just want to ask a question!" I struggled with my foot. The door had it jammed in place and the pressure she was putting on it was painful. Deckard grabbed me and pulled. All I managed to do was lose my shoe, which was wedged firmly in place.

Shoeless, I continued, "We want to know about the Naggian statue. We have information that you have it. That's all we want to know."

Anxiety filled her voice, "Some people already came and took it." I couldn't see much of her, but she had on a loose, white tank top. Her hair was a disheveled mess of curls and her shirt and visible arm were dirty. It was also well-toned.

I groaned loudly. The last thing we needed was more problems.

It had to be them. There was no one else it could be. "Do you have any idea where they were going?"

"They were heading back west. Now go away."

"Can I at least have my shoe back?" I asked, leaning on Deckard and holding up one foot.

She kicked my shoe and it flew out of the door before she slammed it closed. I wiggled my foot back into it.

"At least it doesn't sound like she's going to call anyone?" Deckard offered.

I banged on the door again. "Hey! We have no way to get back!"

"I don't care!"

"Well, it's way too far for us to walk! We're going to be stuck here if there's no other way to get back!"

"Then use the trailer or something! You're not staying here, Nadder!"

I sighed, correcting her in a low voice she had no way of hearing, "Naggian."

Next to me, Deckard shrugged with a meek smirk. Somehow he still managed to feign cheer despite his near-frozen state. Exhaustion seemed to be overtaking him again. His eyes looked ready to close.

"Let's find that trailer," I said. At that moment, Deckard was my responsibility. He wasn't going to have the strength to keep going, and I had to make sure nothing happened to him.

It occurred to me that if she was staying out here alone, she might be frightened by the fact that a Naggian and Geuranian were wandering around outside. It would explain why she was so intent on us leaving. I couldn't imagine that she *wanted* to loan us a trailer.

Being feared was a new and foreign feeling. At my modest size, it had never been an issue before. I felt badly about it, but there was nothing we could do about the fact that we weren't Rhodarens.

The trailer was parked next to one of the sheds. It had a bunch of cords and a tarp with soil and snow on it. Climbing up on the back, I lifted one end of the tarp to shake it off. It sprinkled to the ground. Behind me there was some sort of vehicle that looked similar to the snowmobile, but larger and wider. It was hooked up to the trailer.

"Deckard, why don't you take a nap in the trailer? We can cover up the top."

This was the best I could do and it felt all too little.

"But you don't know how to drive."

"You didn't do that great of a job last time, either, so I'll try this time."

He fumbled over to the vehicle, pointing at it. "You gotta move this to get it to go forward." He gripped the handle, showing me. "And it turns on over here. You sure you're gonna be okay?"

"I'll do my best. Come on."

I tied the tarp to the rails on top of the trailer and got Deckard bundled up in the back. The tarp provided some shelter while the extra clothes we'd brought made for a poor bed. I wished for more, but I couldn't give any without taking my coat off, and I was sure I'd freeze to death quickly if I did that.

When he was strapped in and covered, I jogged over to the front and hopped on the vehicle, playing around with it. I twisted the handle and it lurched forward, stopping when I let go.

Save for a few seconds nearly a year before, it was my first time attempting to drive. I pressed on it slowly, feeling the vehicle vibrate under me as it started to move. At first, I steered too sharply. I wanted to turn a soft corner but would nearly turn ninety degrees. Inexperience left me a poor motorist. I went slow enough that I had time to correct myself. My limbs trembled as I picked up the pace.

It started to glide along the road. Every time I lost confidence I released my grip on the handle and let it slow until I regained control.

Commanding a machine was stressful, but at least it wasn't something huge like a truck. I started to get the hang of it and kept a steady pace on the road. It was the only road leading to the greenhouse, so it had to be the way the other two drove back.

I tried to put together a strategy while I drove. Where would they go now that they had the statue? After I had been driving for a while, their tracks swerved from out of the forest onto the road. Stopping, I rested a foot on the ground and looked into the forest. The faintest outline of their tracks remained. The falling snow had covered up most of them. Why had they gone that way?

Continuing on, I stopped again when I saw smoke in the distance. It looked like it was around that shed we had passed before.

He wanted to make a lot of stops, right? Perhaps we had caught up to them even though we'd been so far behind. If they had gone off the road earlier it explained why we didn't pass them before. I briefly wondered why he wanted to stop so often but it didn't matter. I pulled the trailer over to the side.

Deckard was sound asleep in the back. Worried, I checked to make sure he was warm enough to be safe. His skin was cold, but seemed to be protected enough to keep it from being frostbitten. I didn't want to wake him. Sleep was one thing he desperately needed.

With my worries satisfied for the moment, I crept into the woods and headed towards the shed. The closer I got, the more I could make out. There was a fire outside, but it was controlled, with a steady stream of smoke.

I sneaked closer until I could make out the two people sitting by the fire. They had a cauldron hanging over it and the man was stirring something in it. He sat with his legs crossed. On the other side the old woman was leaning back on something that I couldn't make out. His lympet was out of the bag and sitting next to him.

They looked comfortable, not freezing like Deckard and I were. He poured some of the contents from the cauldron into a bowl and passed it to her. Steam wafted over it. Whatever it was, I wanted it.

His truck was parked by the shed. I crawled as close as I could without being spotted. The lympet flicked an ear and turned her eyes towards me, but she didn't move, and eventually lost interest.

The man lay on his side and put a crinkled, dry stick of food in his mouth. His lympet watched him with disinterest.

"Come on, eat it. It's yummy, see?" he wiggled the piece of food in front of her. She stayed put.

"You look like you have a turd sticking out of your mouth," the woman commented.

"Just roots," his answer was muffled. Pulling it out, he prodded the lympet softly with the lumpy stick. After constant pestering, the lympet finally gave in and bit the other side. He ran a hand down her back and dropped it, encouraging her, "There you go."

The lympet nibbled on the stick as if it were a job but the man seemed satisfied with the results. It was weird seeing someone treating a lympet like some sort of pet. They were always causing trouble in Nagdecht, messing with our gardens and knocking over things. Why someone would want to keep one around? Although his seemed to be quite docile.

"We can stay here for the night if you want. It's not like anyone is going to come by this place," he told the woman.

"The shed doesn't look particularly accommodating."

"We can use the back of the truck. There's plenty of room. With some blankets, it's as good as a hotel room."

"I suppose it's better than driving up the mountain in the dark."

"That settles it then." He stood up. "I'll get it ready."

The man carried sheets from the front and tossed them in the back. Once she'd finished eating, he scooped up the lympet and placed her in the back.

"So what're you planning on doing with that thing anyway?" he asked.

"Actually ..." She stood, rolling her shoulders and stretching her limbs. "I thought perhaps you could help with that. I need to sell it. But I've never sold something like that before. Under the table, you understand."

He leaned on the truck. "You're just selling it? But you own that farm, right? You can get a lot of money for that land. Why bother with this?"

"Never mind that. Do you know how I could get the word out about it? Attract attention?"

"Yeah, sure. You just gotta know the right places. I've been around. You really want to go the underground route instead of an auction or something? You could end up dealing with some rough folks."

"I know. I'm ready." She stayed soft, but resolute.

"That's a small town up there. Would you rather head to a bigger city? You'll find more people. You want to try where you're from?"

"Where I'm from?"

"Edalbag. Where your house was."

"That wasn't my house, but no. I'd like to try the neighboring cities around there. I just have to keep going until I find the right person."

"I dunno what you're up to, Granny, but you're playing with fire there. I won't stop you though." He pulled away from the truck, letting his arms drop loosely and shrugging. "Just point me where you want me to go and I'll go."

He closed the front part of the truck and walked away from the camp with a small phone in hand.

The longer I hid, the more I shivered. They hadn't been shivering at all. Her coat looked nice and thick, and he still had the jacket from before. The warm food must have helped on top of that. I wondered if I would have a chance to snatch some for myself. I waited anxiously for the opportunity.

On the other side of the woods, the man chatted on his phone. His silhouette meandered back and forth with an extra bounce his step. He came back a while later and helped her climb into the back of the truck, before kicking out their fire and putting a lid on top of the cauldron. Mentally I screamed, *Yes!*

By the time he finally climbed into the truck and shut it up, I was practically bouncing in place. I waited to make sure he didn't pop back out before running over to the cauldron. An aura of heat still radiated from it.

I grabbed pot we had brought from the trailer and filled it up, carrying it back.

"Deckard." I opened the back of the trailer and sat on the edge, shaking his leg. "I got something to eat. Don't talk too loud."

"Hnn?" He sat up, rubbing his eyes. He slurred his speech, still half asleep, "What's going on?"

"We're close to them, but they don't know we're here." I dug out a light to get a look at the food. It was a soup packed with all kinds of random looking things. I recognized the potato chunks, but I wasn't sure about everything else. It hardly mattered at the moment. It was hot and I was hungry.

We ate greedily and I lay down next to him. "If we stay here, they shouldn't see us. They're planning on selling the statue, but it doesn't sound like she knows where she wants to go."

"What's the plan?"

"I'm not sure. I didn't see the statue anywhere, but they must have it. We can keep following them."

"Why not just take it now?"

"I'm not sure where they put it. I'm guessing it's in the back of the truck, and they're sleeping in there."

A fight was the last thing I wanted. Deckard could probably hold his own, but I had no training and no experience. Even if we could win a fight with them, I didn't really want to hurt her. After my encounter with the man on the mountain, I was a little less concerned with him.

I nestled under the tarp with Deckard.

"Deckard."

"Yeah?"

"It smells like manure."

"I'm pretty sure this is used to move plants around."

The tarp provided us some protection from the wind. Daydreams of heavy coats danced through my head.

"Deckard."

"Nn?"

"We need to get some thicker coats."

101

"We can go shopping in the morning," he answered wearily.

12
5, 9, 3399
Errday

We slept in the trailer. When I woke up in the morning, I was surprised to see Deckard already up. I slid out from under the tarp and wiped off.

"They headed off a bit ago," he informed me. I wasn't too worried. It was a one-way trip. For the time being, we knew where they were going.

Deckard moved to the vehicle to get on it.

"You're going to drive?" I asked.

"You have a problem with that?"

"I did a pretty good job yesterday." I lifted my eyebrows and folded my arms.

"I'm sure I can do fine if I'm not being chased," he countered.

In all honesty, I didn't mind the opportunity to take a break. As interesting as it had been to drive, it was also nerve-racking. I'd constantly worried about losing control. Sitting tensed up had been tiring.

"What about the trailer? Should we take it with us?" he asked.

"We could use it to sleep on again."

"We'll be driving back up that mountain, and probably need to get near that town again."

I put a finger to my chin, thinking.

"You're right. We could leave the trailer by the shed down here. It'll probably be easier navigating that path without it."

After unhooking the trailer by the shed, we continued on. I held onto Deckard from behind. He went slower this time, maintaining control. It was snowing, and I wondered if it would be like that the entire time we were here.

While we were heading up the mountain I glanced down the side that we had tumbled down from. It was a long, steep fall. I could see how futile it had been to try and catch myself. The entire incident was a blur in my head.

It was still daytime when we got to the town, which left us in a conundrum. We needed to catch up to the other two, but we couldn't go into town. We parked a distance from it, taking a seat in the snow.

"She said she wanted to sell it, but not in a legit way. And she wanted to attract attention. I wonder how Rhodarens do that. Maybe a bar? That's where she posted something before."

"There's going to be a lot of bars."

"Maybe we need to find the shadier areas."

"Well, you can usually tell how safe a place is by the way it looks."

"In Nagdecht, dangerous areas usually have a lot of stuff open late at night," I suggested.

"So you think we should look for areas that are lit up at night?"

"Maybe." I nodded.

"That comes with the problem of not being seen."

I sighed. "We'll figure out something."

I wished I understood Rhodarens. If I did, I'd have a much better idea where they would go.

"Hey, couldn't we call the places?" I asked. I dug into my bag and pulled out the small phone.

He smiled. "Good idea. Then we just need numbers."

We went through what little food we had left and worked on plans to look up businesses. By the time night rolled around, we were veritable ice cubes. We tried to make jokes and laugh it off. Deckard even

104

joked around suggesting that we should snuggle. But even sitting close to each other wasn't enough to stave off the cold. It was relentless, never giving us a moment of relief.

I was glad when evening fell and we could make a move. Images of warm buildings filled my mind.

We sneaked into town and used the access panel to look up the bars. There were only a few. I looked up the nearest cities, too, since they were discussing traveling around to sell it.

Relief came when we broke into a building. I shook off my coat. Snow drifted to the floor, dotting it with dozens of droplets. Starting from the top of our list and working our way down, we began making calls and asked if anyone had been trying to sell anything.

They had stopped by one of the bars but hadn't sold it. I asked if they knew where they were going next and they only had a vague idea. They gave me "Delmar's" number, but I didn't think calling them directly would work.

While I was making notes, Deckard whispered to me, "Hey."

"Yeah?"

"I've been thinking. If she's trying to sell that thing, won't they have to stay in one place for a bit? In order to get a response from potential buyers?"

"I guess you're right. Maybe we won't have to run around that much. Anyway, she seemed to want to keep around that one city where the guy lived for some reason, so we have some idea of where they'll be going."

Things were starting to look up. We knew where the statue was, who had it, and where they were going. Thinking about all the positives cheered me up as I scribbled out my own personal map. We just had to plan how to get the statue from them. They probably wouldn't carry it into the bars with them. They'd either leave it in the truck or store it somewhere.

"Think we should go see if we spot that truck by the bar? Maybe we could grab the statue off the back while they're inside."

"We could try it if you want, but that means going back outside." Deckard was lounging in a seat with his feet up on a table and his hands behind his head.

"All right, let's get our priorities straight." I started a list. "Food. Statue. Coats."

"We can see if they have any food stashed here," he suggested.

The business we had broken into looked like a dental office. We searched the reception area. There wasn't much. Someone had left half a package of cookies and that was it.

It was better than nothing, so we took it and left. We made our way to the bar, taking dark streets until we found it. The familiar truck was outside. No one was in it, so we crouched and slunk around to the back.

I opened it up to find nothing but blankets.

"Did they take it inside?" I asked Deckard.

He nodded his head towards the other side of the street. "We could hide and see when they come out."

Eventually they came out, but once again there was no box. It was missing.

"Where to now?" Delmar asked as he rounded the truck to the driver's side.

The old woman answered confidently, "They have my information. We should be able to move on."

That posed a whole new problem. Figuring out where they put the box.

We pondered our options. We could either sneak into the back of their truck or go back for the snowmobile. If we sneaked in the back of their truck, we wouldn't lose them, but they might find us. If we went back for our vehicle we might lose them. There wasn't much time to decide.

"I've got their number," I whispered to Deckard. "If we have to, we can try to track them with that."

He acknowledged me with a nod before we made our way back to the snowmobile. That still left the problem of keeping warm and getting more food, but it was a start. We called the bar again in the morning. This time Deckard did the speaking, and we were informed that the two had left for the city.

With a name and a direction, we pursued them. We spent the days hiding out and making the occasional call to bars, searching for updates. It wasn't until a few days later that we got a bite. We called to ask if someone had been interested in selling a statue, and the person told us that it had already been sold. Stranger yet, when we insisted on knowing where they went she said it sounded like they were going to a forest, but she didn't know which one.

"How are we going to find that out?" Deckard asked.

"We already know," I told him. "The box was missing when they went to the first town. They had hid it somewhere by those mountains and hills. Come on, let's hurry back!"

Hours passed on the drive back to the forest that I hated so much at night. The single road served as a lucky break again. They only had one way to go and we were able to find and begin following their tracks into the forest.

It seemed like it would be another day of tracking them down. Until we heard the gunshots.

13

5, 10, 3399
Waddersday

People came to ask about the statue. Delmar waited outside of the room while she tried to make a deal. The room was dim with a single lamp in the corner. It bathed the room in an orange glow. She sat at a wooden table with her hands folded on it. Her cane was leaning against it by her chair.

A couple came in. She knew immediately she wasn't interested in selling it to them. They sat across from her on the other side of the table.

"We heard that you have possession of an old statue. We'd be interested in buying and preserving it," the woman said.

"I'm sorry, I'm not interested in selling it to you," she answered. She had been straightforward in her answers to people. She didn't want to waste time.

Taken aback by the quick, dismissive answer, she leaned forward and persisted, "If it's a matter of money, we'd gladly offer more."

"No, thank you. I'm afraid I'm not interested," she remained firm. "Please tell them to send in the next person."

She looked at the man with her, surprise and disappointment written on their faces. They got up and left abruptly, closing the door roughly behind them. Taking a deep breath, she sighed, waiting.

She caught a glimpse of Delmar leaning outside the door when it opened again. A new prospect entered. A woman in a thick, blue coat that covered almost everything. Again, she knew that she wasn't interested in selling to this person.

"I'm sorry, I'm not interested," she said before the woman had a chance to sit down. "Can you please send in the next person?"

"You haven't even talked to me yet," the woman replied, agitated.

"I know, but I've already decided. I'd like to see who else there is."

"Do you have a problem with me?" She slapped a hand on the table, leaning over it.

Breigah leaned back, but remained calm. She knew she would have to deal with rougher people if she intended to sell the statue this way.

"No, I'm just looking for something specific," she explained.

"And how do you know I'm not 'something specific'?" she demanded.

"Please, I'm not interested in arguing. I'd just like to move on."

"Well I'd like some better answers!" She reached under her coat. With a gasp, Breigah reached under her own coat. Her fingers touched the handle of the cold, metal weapon. She shoved the chair back, grabbing its arm, and pushing herself to her feet as the woman approached.

"Hey!"

The man called from the other side of the door. He threw it open and rushed in. Breigah moved around to the opposite side of the table, fingers still gripping the handle of the hidden weapon as Delmar sprinted in to interfere.

The woman spun to face him. He grabbed her arm and they wrestled.

"We could use some help in here!" he yelled towards the hallway as he struggled to hold her still.

Employees of the bar ran in to help and dragged the woman out. Breigah loosened her grip on her gun, holding a hand to her chest and breathing heavily.

"You all right, Granny?" Delmar turned to her after watching the staff leave.

"Yes. I've just never dealt with something like that before."

"Told you it'd be dangerous. Sure you don't want to look for a more legit route?" Folding his arms, he gave her a serious look.

"No, I think this is the best way."

"Some of those people are willing to offer a lot more money than you put it up for, you know. You should find a good deal."

"I'll know when I find what I'm looking for," she assured him. "Please wait outside and give me a moment. That was very … stressful."

He quirked a brow at her and turned to walk back out of the door.

She fell back into her seat. Her heart was racing. She was thankful the woman hadn't reached her with the knife. She hadn't wanted to use the gun.

She waited for her heart to settle before calling out to the man, "Please send the next person in."

14
5, 11, 3399
Windsday

A new city, a new bar. They had spread the word again, and paid a small fine to make use of a back room. She insisted on staying alone in the room despite Delmar asking if she wanted him to stay inside. He was close enough, if she needed him.

An assortment of characters came through the room, both normal and shady. She had no interest in any of them and rejected their offers promptly.

She stayed calm until a familiar face walked in. Her heart hardened. Her expression became grave.

"So I hear you've got something really rare, but you've been reluctant to part with it," he started as he took a seat opposite her.

"I haven't gotten an interesting enough offer yet," she answered, forcing herself to remain calm.

"What kind of offer are you looking for?" He slung an arm over the back of his chair. She wrinkled her nose, disgusted by his lax attitude.

"I suppose the right amount of money and perhaps some unique kitchenware or home décor might do the trick," she answered. She had no interest in either, but she didn't want to rouse his suspicions.

"I could throw in a little more money, and I've got some pretty unique plates you might be interested in. They're real pieces of fine art," he offered.

She stayed quiet for a moment, as if mulling it over. She didn't want to sound too eager.

"Need to see them?"

She didn't want to waste time, but she had to remain calm. "Yes. Can you bring them here tonight?"

"I don't live far. I could grab them and be back in half an hour," he answered.

"All right then. What is your name? I'll let them know to let you come back," she explained.

"Holf," he answered. "And you?"

"You can just call me 'Grandma.' Everyone else does," she told him, cringing at the thought of him calling her that.

"All right then, Grandma, I'll be back soon."

He left the room. She stood from her spot, walking to the door with the cane and opening it to see Delmar.

"I've found the one," she told him. "He goes by Holf. You can let him inside again when he comes back."

"Really? Are you sure you're going to sell it to him? He doesn't look like he has as much as some of the other people did."

"Don't worry about that. When he comes back, I'm going to ask him to follow us there."

"I can just give him a ride with us."

"I don't want to sit next to him," she answered. Her frown was so deep that he wondered if it would leave a permanent mark on her face.

"What's going on here, Granny?"

"Don't worry about it. When everything is settled, you can have the farm."

He pursed his lips. It was a big payout for his short service, but that made it suspicious. Something else was going on, but he didn't know what.

The man returned near half an hour later and went straight to the back room. He placed the plates on the table for her to see. They were antiques, both old and in good condition. She glared down at them. She traced a finger along one of the edges and picked it up, feigning interest.

"You must have paid quite a bit for these," she said, a hint of scorn in her voice.

"They're legit, and in good condition. You'll have a hard time finding another set in this shape," he built them up, praising them. She knew he was simply trying to convince her more that it would be a good trade.

"You're quite right about that. It seems we have a deal," she agreed.

"Great. Then when can I pick up the statue?"

"We'll have to drive a distance to get it. Would you be able to follow us?"

"I don't have anything myself, but I can rent something."

"Good. We'll head out in the morning. The man at the door can give you directions where to meet if you get lost."

She stood, leaving the plates behind and heading out the door. She ignored Delmar and continued by. She was too tense to engage him in conversation.

The night dragged on and she felt as if the next morning would never come. She spent the rest of her time in a small room they rented nearby. Delmar stayed with her, but they avoided conversing. He once paused at the door to the wash room, looking back at her as if ready to attempt conversation, but he decided against it and went inside to clean up.

She sat on the edge of her bed, cane standing tall in front of her as she leaned on it. Her chin rested on the back of her hands. She felt as if she stared at the covered window for hours before she finally pulled herself up and prepared for bed.

She woke early and paced around the room until Delmar got up. He cooked a simple breakfast for them both. Though she didn't feel like eating, she knew she had to, and she forced her way through the meal, thanking him quietly after.

They met the man by a nearby cart pickup. He had rented a hefty snowmobile that could shelter him from the wind and snow. She knew they didn't require a license to drive and were fairly common compared to other vehicles.

She boarded the truck expecting, wanting silence, but as her companion had done before, he flipped on the radio. She cringed. The joyous music didn't fit her tense mood, nor did his cheerful singing along. It was going to be a long, long ride.

15

Two loud bangs rang through the air. A sparse flock of birds flew by. Deckard stopped the vehicle and planted his foot on the ground.

"What was that?" I asked. Even though I knew what it was, I wanted him to confirm my thoughts.

"It was gunfire," he said.

For a few tense moments, we stayed in place. Was Deckard weighing whether we should approach or not, like I was? I wanted to know what was going on. I also wanted to live.

"Deckard." I grabbed his arm. "Neither of them had a gun. Whoever they brought out here must have shot them!"

The outlook for our mission was changing rapidly.

"Calm down, we don't know if anyone is shot yet," he answered.

He was right. We didn't know if anyone was dead or alive yet. Or injured.

"We have to go see if they're okay," I told him. The thought of someone stumbling around out there, possibly fatally injured, made me sick. If they were hurt, they would be far from help. Two shots meant they could both be … I clenched my jaw.

"It's hard to tell which direction it came from …" he mumbled, before he lifted his foot and began driving again. We rode through the trees at a crawl, keeping our eyes peeled. To our left, I saw something large and brown in the distance. I nudged Deckard and pointed him towards it.

It was their truck and another snowmobile. No one else was around. We rushed over to investigate.

"No blood," Deckard said as he looked around.

"They might have been chased," I told him.

He pointed at some mashed up clumps of snow. "The snow is messy around here."

At the base of a tree, it looked like someone had kicked around the snow. Some wood splinters were mixed in, and I turned up my eyes. It was difficult to see on the dark bark, but there was a hole in the tree.

"A bullet hole!" I announced, touching it. It confirmed for me what was happening. Someone was taking shots at them.

Deckard put a hand on the trunk and glanced behind us. His eyes scanned the ground. He pointed, moving his finger as he spoke. "It looks like they ran this way. They probably kept going in this direction somewhere."

Small clues were scattered in the snow. Staying close to each other, we walked in that direction. In my panicked state, I couldn't keep accurate track of time. It felt like we walked for a long time, but it could have been twenty minutes or less.

We came on an odd sight while searching. The familiar lympet was hobbling around in the forested area alone. Deckard and I exchanged glances. She stopped, looking up at us and letting out a small mewl. With her stumpy short legs, she had to push her way through the snow. She turned around and looked back at us, mewling once more. She seemed to want us to follow her, so we did. I watched her take shaky, slow steps and realized something. She wasn't a lazy animal. She was old. Even walking seemed to be a struggle for her.

She led us along through the trees. I couldn't tell if she was waiting for us to follow or if she just couldn't go any faster. The flat land began curving up into one of the hills until we were climbing up a mountain path formed by nature. It narrowed and was rocky and unstable.

We knew it when we reached our destination. Ahead of us the path had crumbled. Down the fallen path, Delmar was lying in a pile of rocks. More notably, a branch was going straight through his leg. It was the leafless branch of a tree that had died on the mountainside. I winced at the sight. I *knew* those trees were out to get us.

The branch went through his thigh, pinning him sideways. He held himself up on his arms. The lympet stuck two paws down the side as if she was getting ready to jump, but she slipped and rolled, crashing to the bottom. She staggered over to her master and sat by his head. A tiny mewl reached my ears. He turned as far as he could to look over his shoulder up at us.

He heaved a sigh, reaching to pet her head. "You tried."

Deckard and I looked at each other. We couldn't leave him there. I sat by the pit and carefully scaled the rocks to get a better look at the situation. He glared over his shoulder at me as I approached and drew his lympet closer to his chest. I felt badly for her. She had put all of her strength into finding him help, but she didn't know what "Rhodaren," "Geuranian," and "Naggian" meant. She saw people and she brought people.

I knelt down next to him. The branch wasn't perfectly straight, and it was rooted in the ground. I yelled up at Deckard, "I think we'll have to cut him out."

He climbed down and we sorted through our bags to find something to use. I tried to make conversation while Deckard looked for something to cut with. "So, the ground collapsed under you."

"Right," he answered curtly with his arm around the lympet.

"How did you end up almost on your back like this?" I asked. He was on his side, but it seemed odd that he would end up that way instead of trying to catch himself.

"I was barely able to hold her up," he said. I paused.

"'Her' ... the lympet?" I furrowed my brows, picturing it in my head. The road collapsed. He began falling forward. Instead of catching himself he grabbed the lympet. "Why would you do that? You could have broken your back!"

"I would have squished her if I didn't!" he snapped back.

I imagined it again. The lympet had always been in a bag on his side. I glanced up at the road and noted the direction we had come. She always hung on his left side. When the road collapsed he would have been falling on his left side. He grabbed her and was barely able to twist around to hold her up, so that he ended up falling on his back left side. Somehow it made sense to this lympet-obsessed Rhodaren. Letting something happen to her wasn't an option.

Laid out in front of Deckard were some knives. They were all we had. A saw would have been nice, but neither of us had the foresight to pack one.

Deckard picked up one of the knives. I tossed my extra jacket on the ground and he lay on it, reaching under the Rhodaren and sawing at the branch. He gritted his teeth and hissed as the branch wiggled in his leg. It wasn't the best tool for cutting through the branch, so after a few minutes Deckard sat up and I took his place, using all off my strength to keep cutting. I held it in one hand to keep it steady and cut with the other.

There was a snap when the knife finally made it through. I accidentally jerked the branch when it suddenly came loose, prompting a pained yelp from the man. I flinched, pulling my hand away. He reached down to hold the branch in place, panting.

We got him on his back and cut off the other end. The first end by the ground had been about an inch thick, and the part on the other side was around half the width. I tried to ignore the wet substance going down the branch.

Once we'd cut the branch into something more manageable, we were able to carry him. Even though he attempted to walk it was impossible in his condition. He couldn't use his leg at all and groaned in pain when he tried. Deckard lifted him from under his armpits and I helped guide him back up the rocks. The man was holding onto his lympet, which was probably for the best. I wasn't any more certain about her ability to walk than I was about his.

Pushing through despite sore muscles, we carried him back to his truck. I kept my eyes averted from the wound. It went through his inner thigh and was poking out the other end. We couldn't leave it there.

"Deckard!" I looked to him. "You're in the army, you should have some medical training. What should we do?"

He stared at me wide-eyed.

My expression dropped. "… You didn't pay attention in training, did you?"

"I never really thought I'd be doing it."

I threw my hands in the air. "Why can't you ever just pay attention?" No matter what it was, he always seemed to be too lazy to bother.

"I figured that I'd be surrounded by people who knew how to do it better than me anyway! It's not like you know, either!"

"But I'm not a soldier!"

"I didn't want to be!"

"Well, we have to do something! We can't just leave a giant branch sticking out of him!"

"Just be quiet, I'm trying to think!"

"Look, I'm going to start cleaning it," I told him. I searched for something to use as a rag.

"Hold on, get it higher than his head," Deckard said.

He was lying down in the back of the truck and we perched his leg on a pile of sheets. It was a start at least. I wiped off the area on his leg, and cut away loose bark and bumps from the branch, working on making it straight and clean.

"How are we going to get it out?" I asked, staring at Deckard with wide eyes.

"I don't know. I mean, you're not supposed to usually, but it's not like there's a hospital here." He rubbed the back of his neck as he looked at the leg.

"But he can't just walk around with a branch in his leg!"

Deckard lifted his hands up in a surrender position. "I don't know what to do about it! We could just make it worse."

"Can't we bandage it or something?"

"Damnit, I don't have all day to listen to you two," the man grumbled. He grabbed the branch and tugged. He clenched his jaw and groaned in pain as he pulled, moving it about an inch. His entire arm shook from the strain before he stopped, panting heavily. Beads of sweat formed on his forehead despite the weather.

I waved my hands to signal him to stop, panicking. "Okay, okay!" I hesitantly reached for the branch. It was unlikely he could pull the whole thing out by himself, but he might try, and I could only imagine how painful that was.

"Stay still," I told him. With a tight grip on the branch I started pulling on it, careful to keep it straight. Deckard started ripping up some of the sheets.

Keeping my hand steady was a challenge. My body wanted to shake as much as the man did. He slammed his hand on the floor of the truck. I was terrified of making a mistake and wanted to stop but I kept going. With one hand on his inner thigh, I felt it slowly squeeze through. When it got to the end it popped out suddenly. I glanced at it for a second before throwing it away from me. Tears had welled up in his eyes and his teeth were clenched so tight I wondered if he'd broken any.

Deckard had the sense to shove something in his mouth before he wiped him off then started wrapping his leg up. There was blood, but I was surprised there wasn't more. I let my body fall into tremors now that I wasn't touching him anymore. The makeshift bandages were wound around him tightly. When Deckard was finally done, the man tilted his head back in a feverish sweat. He was hyperventilating, his fingers attempting to break through the metal floor.

We did a bad job. I already knew it. Even if I pulled it out straight, we didn't have any gloves, or disinfectant, or even real bandages. But we stopped the bleeding for the moment. I took a deep breath. It seemed like he would be okay for now.

More gunshots rang out in the air and snapped my mind back to attention. The old woman was still out there somewhere.

I leaned over him, asking urgently, "Hey, where's that woman?"

"Not sure. I was following them when the road gave way. She's somewhere farther along," he said.

"Come on." I scooted out of the back of the truck. "We have to go get her before she's caught!"

"Before she's caught?" the Rhodaren asked.

"Yeah," I answered. "By whoever was shooting at you guys."

He pushed himself up despite the obvious pain it was causing him. "We weren't being shot at. She was the one who pulled out a gun."

I stopped, standing next to the end of the truck. That was the last thing I expected. "She ... was?"

"We were standing around getting ready to dig up the box when she pulled out a gun and started shooting at him. He ran off," he waved his arms in the direction they had gone, "and she chased after him."

"What? Why?"

"I don't know. She ran off without me. Didn't tell me a thing," he answered, sliding towards the back of the truck. He looked back at the lympet, pointing down. "You stay here."

The Rhodaren got onto his feet. He put all of his weight on one leg while leaning on the truck. His resilience stunned me.

"You can't run around like that!" I snapped at him.

"Like hell am I sitting around here. Get me a stick or something."

He ended up holding Deckard for support since we couldn't find anything sturdy enough for him to use. Making our way back to where we found him was slow going. No matter how slowly I went, he and Deckard seemed to be going slower, so I was always a pace ahead.

When we edged across the break in the road, I took extra care. We only had about a foot of space to balance on. The man stubbornly insisted on coming. I worried about his leg failing him every second he was edging across. Somehow he managed to make it and we traveled up the hill. The road expanded into a wide, bumpy area at the top. Behind us, I could see that we had climbed about four or five stories higher than where we had started.

We trudged on until we spotted something dark lying in the snow. I ran ahead first, almost forgetting that the other two would take a while to join me. The woman was lying in the snow, but not in the condition I expected. She lay on her back with a hand on her stomach. Blood covered her hand, and her shirt and coat were soaked all around her stomach. A shovel was lying on the ground several yards away from her.

I rushed over and knelt by her. The other two hobbled closer. "Quick, we have to do something!"

I glanced around for something to press on the wound. The Rhodaren man took a seat nearby and Deckard joined me. She was still breathing. I pulled up her shirt to see the wound. The bullet had gone through her abdomen.

"Hurry up!" I shouted at them both. She couldn't have much time left.

"There's nothing we can do," Delmar answered.

"But we have to do something!"

"She's been shot in the gut. There's too many organs that are probably torn up, and we're too far from any hospitals. There's nothing we can do about it. She's as good as dead."

Dread washed over me. I'd never watched someone die. Even when I was close to death, I hadn't seen it. I felt a strong urge to try and do something even if it was futile. I pressed down on her wound with my bare hands. Her chest heaved when she took in breaths. Deckard crawled to her other side.

"Holf," she murmured weakly.

"Do something!" I yelled at Deckard, but he seemed just as flustered as I was.

"I don't think we can." We sat, frozen literally and figuratively. I couldn't think of a single thing to do to besides put pressure on the wound. A baritone voice

sung something quietly nearby. I didn't register any of the words. It was some sort of murmuring in the background.

"We can't just sit here!" I screamed, but my pleas did nothing to change our circumstances.

My eyes flitted from Deckard to Delmar behind us. The singing was coming from him. He held his head down with a hand to his forehead.

"This is no time for singing!" I barked at him. He stopped, lowered his hand and glared at me without a word.

My breathing was rapid. I looked back at her. It took a moment to register that she wasn't breathing anymore. For a moment that took far too long, I stared at her, waiting to see her chest move again. It didn't.

I finally forced myself away, stumbling and vomiting in the bushes. Nausea overwhelmed me. I stuck my hands into the snow and washed them off as much as I could. When I looked back Delmar was kneeling by her and rifling through her possessions.

"What are you doing?!" I yelled at him as I rushed over to stop him.

"She doesn't need any of this anymore. Besides, there might be some clue where to go." He pulled out a pile of letters, flipping them over to glance at both sides.

"You shouldn't just go through her stuff!"

"I don't know about you, but I want to know what's going on here." He sorted through it. "It looks like the paperwork on the statue is missing." I quieted. I did want to find out, but it felt wrong.

"Should we bury her?" Deckard asked.

"There is a shovel," I said.

"No, I'll tell the authorities about it later. They can come get her. We should get back to the truck."

"We're just leaving?"

127

"I'll tell you one thing. I don't see her gun, so I'm leaving."

His ominous words struck me hard. The gun had slipped my mind, but he was right. It wasn't there.

He took hold of her cane and climbed to his feet. We made our way back to the truck with the shovel, letters and her cane. Delmar sat on the back. I felt strangely empty. Watching someone die, helpless to do anything about it, left me flustered. Sitting next to him, I stared down at the ground. What were we supposed to do now?

"I didn't even know her name," I lamented aloud.

"Breigah," he answered simply.

"Speaking of which," Deckard butted in, "we don't really know each other, either." He had his hands shoved in his pockets and he was failing at acting casual, shifting his weight from one leg to another.

"Delmar," he answered, then his eyes turned to the lympet. "And she's Feenie."

"I'm Leander."

"Deckard."

Silence fell over us. After a second, I noticed the other snowmobile was gone and felt uneasy that someone had been there in our absence. I moved closer to Deckard.

"What about the statue? Don't you know where it is?" I asked. I felt badly asking. It seemed callous after just seeing her die.

"Yeah." He gestured. "We buried it over there. She wanted to make sure no one found it before she was ready."

"Deckard?" I hesitantly looked at him. I wasn't sure if considering it was even okay.

He shrugged. "We're here anyway?"

We took the shovel over with Delmar directing us and began digging. It didn't take long to get to the

128

box and we pulled it up. But when we opened it there was only a rock inside.

"What is this?" I demanded.

"What?" Delmar asked.

"There's just a rock in here."

"There is?" He sounded surprised.

"Yeah." I looked to him. "Where's the statue?"

He shrugged, "I don't know, she's the one who found it. Or, found that box at least. But she had the paperwork to go with it."

"You mean the papers she took from me?"

"No, the real ones, not copies."

"She had the real paperwork but not the statue?" I asked.

"Maybe she had it somewhere else. I don't know." He grew agitated as we discussed it. Stress, and a lack of answers, was getting to all of us.

There didn't seem to be any point in taking the box or the rock. I tossed the shovel in the back of the truck. The lympet was still inside lying down. Deckard stood next to me with his hands shoved in his pockets.

"All right, I'm no bum." Delmar pushed off of the back, kneeling in front of us. "You saved my life and I owe you."

The statement came straight out of nowhere. I looked to Deckard and he shrugged, answering, "Must be a Rhodaren thing."

"I'm not surprised Nadders don't know about honor." Delmar huffed.

"Naggian. And we have plenty of honor!" I snapped back.

He attempted to stand up. His leg trembled terribly when he put weight on it.

"Give me a minute," he said as he slowly worked his way up from a kneeling position, trying to keep weight off the injured one. He stabbed the ground with the cane and forced himself up. I wanted to help him, but held off.

"What was that about?" I asked.

"Rhodarens pay off their debts. So what is it that you need?" he asked.

I furrowed my brows, looking to Deckard. After running around in the snow and even sticking my hands in it there was one thing at the forefront of my mind. "Someplace warm?"

"Fair enough. I'm renting a place back in Bemler. I can get you guys over there, get this thing treated and report the body." Before I had a chance to respond, he turned to his lympet. "Feenie, over here."

She toddled over, and he packed her away in his bag.

"Stay in the back so no one sees you," he ordered us. We complied. In the back of my mind, I feared that he would turn us in, but I wanted to relax. Loading the snowmobile into the back, we climbed in and were on our way.

I mentally compared Delmar and Deckard while sitting in the dark. Rhodarens and Geuranians were supposed to be closely related, but they sure didn't look it. Deckard was pale, like someone who was deathly ill. Delmar was dark, like someone who had been fried in the sun. "Burnt" umber – aptly named. His nose and ears had a curve to them while Deckard's were straight. Then there was the size difference. Deckard was fitter, more like a Naggian, while Delmar looked frighteningly large. The blue eyes were different from Delmar's dark brown, too. I looked more like Deckard than Delmar did.

Any connection the two races had seemed to be wiped away. Deckard and I had more in common, being closer to the same size and not contrasting quite as much with each other. Briefly, I wondered if our assessment of their genes was inaccurate somehow, but historically it made sense. Nagdecht had united as one kingdom thousands of years ago, taking over the eastern side of the continent. Long after that, Rhodaren had decided to unite as well, and it was only then that Geuranians took up arms and they became two defined, separate countries. Before that, they interacted a lot.

I let out one amused huff under my breath. Geuranians had never stopped fighting since the beginning. They were always troublemakers. Clinging to my coat, I waited to arrive at our destination.

16

5, 12, 3399
Firsday

Delmar drove us back to the small home that he had stayed at before. He parked the backside of the truck close to the door so we could slip out and into the house.

Getting inside the home was a lifesaver. Warm air immediately embraced me. I found a sink and rinsed off, ready to be rid of every drop of blood. Delmar didn't stay long. He drove off to get treated and report the murder, leaving us alone in the house.

It was my first time inside a genuine Rhodaren house. It had wood panels and a wood floor. At first, I kept to myself and left his things alone. The more my eyes meandered, though, the more I became intrigued. I wandered around the house, studying everything. Their furnishings were more rustic than ours. By the wall, there was a table with a screen sitting on top of it. I wasn't sure what it was for.

I found the washroom, and was ready for a shower, when I saw something horrifying nearby. A toilet. I glanced between the two in disbelief. There wasn't even a wall separating them. Even the cheapest places at least had that much. It was going to be hard showering when I could see that thing a couple of feet away.

Searching through the rest of the bathroom … or should it be called a washroom? I wasn't sure. But I looked around and found a stack of towels and some string sturdy enough to hold them. I tied the string up to some fixtures next to the shower and hung the towels over it, creating a barrier between the shower and the intruding toilet.

It was the best I could do. I still had some qualms about it, but tried to ignore them. Even if I didn't have another set of clothes, I still wanted to get what was left of the blood and dirt off. The hot water felt good on my skin, and once I got out, Deckard took a turn.

I spent the time alone looking over the furniture and knick-knacks around the home. It had a surprisingly warm feel. The living room had a miniature chandelier. It was the fanciest thing in the house. For seating, it had a long beige couch and a small matching one. There was a bookcase. The lower shelves had books and the top shelf had a pile of random items. On top was a dagger inside of a case. When I opened it to take a peek it had small chains to hang it on the wall.

Satisfied with my sleuthing, or just too tired to keep going, I lay back on the smaller couch. Not long after, Deckard came out of the shower and plopped down on the other sofa. For once, we relaxed in comfort. Physically. My mind was filled with images of that woman dying. Somehow it felt like we should have been able to do something. I don't know what, but something.

I tried to think of other things. The statue. Deckard. What Rhodarens were like. But it all kept coming back to her. She had said something when she died – like a name. What did it mean? What had she done with the statue? Not even Delmar seemed to know. Why did she have a gun? And why was she trying to shoot that other guy?

It was a confusing, stressful situation that I wished I had no part of.

It felt like an eternity before Delmar returned. A part of my mind was eased when he didn't come back with police officers. His pants were ripped and he had cleaner bandages under them. He still used the cane to support his weight. Lowering his bag to the ground after he came in, he let the lympet out. She sat where he left her, only her tail flicking up and down.

"How can you do that?" I asked.

"Do what?"

"How are you walking around out there with ripped up pants? Aren't you freezing?"

He glanced behind him, out the window. "It's not that cold out right now."

"Not that cold out? It's snowing out there!"

"It's almost always snowing. It's not bad right now."

He hobbled over to his kitchen, pulling out a drink from the refrigerator. His fridge was a monster, looking like it could pack enough food for a family of five. It was just a bit taller than him, wide, and jutted out farther than the counter around it did.

"So what's your story?" he asked.

"Me?"

"A Nadder and a Geuranian in the middle of Rhodaren. There's gotta be a story."

"That statue happens to be from ancient Nagdecht. It belongs to us, and I'm going to bring it back," I explained.

"And the Geuranian?"

I smirked. "He's just a troublemaker."

"You're the troublemaker," Deckard bantered back under his breath.

"All right then. So what's your plan of action?"

"Right now? I'd really like something warmer to wear. My coat doesn't seem to cut it. After that …" I pondered it. We had come for the statue, but the woman's death had taken us by surprise. And she left us a dying message. It felt wrong to ignore her. "You told the police about that woman, right?"

135

"Yeah. I reported it anonymously."

"Do you think they'll find the guy who killed her?"

He shrugged. "They don't have a ton to go on."

"She said something before she died."

"Holf," he repeated.

"It sounds like a name."

"So you want to figure out what she was up to?"

"I still want to find the statue, but I can't just forget her ... We could at least find out who that person is. Do you have any idea?" He had spent the most time with her, so he would have the most information.

"None, we only know what he looks like. I was just following directions, but I do know someplace we can look." He paused. "Tomorrow."

I wasn't going to argue with him on that. Sleep looked promising.

I tried to focus on something more positive. I had brought some money, and with a Rhodaren here I could possibly get something.

"Hey." I grabbed his attention as he leaned on the counter and finished his drink. "I have some money. Maybe you can get something for me?"

"Like what?"

"I have a friend who is really into foreign stuff. Maybe some Rhodaren necklaces or something? And the coats." I dug into my bag and fetched my satchel of coins. They were from Nagdecht, but their value was based on the metal they were made of. It was the only way the three countries could manage any trade with each other.

He downed his drink, and before he limped over, I got up and handed him the bag. He was injured, it wouldn't be right to make him run around unnecessarily.

He opened it up and held up one of the coins, examining it. "Real Nadder coins… You don't see these often."

"I see them all the time," I responded.

He raised his brows at me, giving me a queer look. Realizing the stupidity of my statement, I kept talking to brush it aside, "They're not tendecks or anything, but it should be enough for something nice."

"You mean dendecks?" he asked.

I furrowed my brows and repeated, "Tendecks."

"You're saying it funny. It's dendecks."

"It's not 'dendecks.' It's tendecks," I said lowly, irritated by his correction.

"No, it's dendecks."

The stubborn man wouldn't let it drop. I looked to Deckard, who seemed to be shying away from the debate on the couch. Throwing a hand up to gesture towards Delmar, I told him, "It's tendecks! Tell him, Deckard."

"Ah, actually," his voice was quieter than normal, "we say … dendecks."

"See?" Delmar lifted his chin in victory.

Surprised by Deckard taking his side, I refused to back down, knowing they were wrong. "Well, you're both wrong! It's tendecks! 'Dendecks' doesn't even make any sense because it's 'ten tecks.'" It was simple when it came down to it. One teck was one hundred shills, and tendecks was one thousand shills. It was an obvious mashing of words.

He hummed thoughtfully, glancing away. "I never thought about that." Feeling relieved that he seemed to be seeing reason, I started to settle down before he added, "But it's still dendecks. And it's 'decks,' not 'tecks.'" I lowered my ears and growled in frustration at him.

Then he smirked, twirling the bag in his hand before pocketing it. "I bet there's someone who would be interested in having genuine Nadder coins. Give them all to me and I can buy that stuff, no problem."

"Naggians."

"What?"

"It's what we're called. Naggians."

"Never heard of it."

"You have now."

"Whatever. I'm going to get some sleep. We're heading to the other house tomorrow."

"Don't forget the coats and stuff."

"I won't."

"And how about some food?"

He gestured at the refrigerator. "Help yourselves."

I took a look at his fridge. The doors were packed with condiments and he had different things wrapped up inside. I peeked under the foil of a bowl and saw some strange, goopy-looking noodle things. I didn't know what they were, so I wrapped it back up. A couple of pieces of already cooked meat sat on a shelf. There was some plain looking bread and a jug of some sort of red liquid. In the corner on the kitchen counter, there was a pile of biscuits wrapped in plastic.

It was strange to see bread in the refrigerator. I wasn't sure how old the meat was and felt suspicious of its intentions towards my stomach. Though oddly bright colored, the drink was the least peculiar thing. I poured a bit into a cup to see what it was. It had a strange sweetness to it, as if someone had poured sugar in it. It made me scrunch up my face.

As plain as it was, the bread was at least recognizable. No nuts, no fruit, no topping. It was a light tan color all the way around. I took a test bite of the corner. Bland. There had to be a topping for it, so I browsed through the condiments to find what he used.

A jar filled with a brown and purple jam sat on the side of the door. I wasn't sure about it, though.

"Hey," I called for him. "What do you put on this?" I held up the piece of bread.

"Cheese is fine."

"Just cheese?"

"Yeah, just grill it with cheese."

It sounded strange. I gave the bread a quizzical look as if waiting for it to grill itself. "I've never done that before."

He let out a hefty sigh. "Give me a minute."

A bit later he came back and put a pan on the stove. He melted some butter in it and tossed the bread in with some square, plastic-looking pieces of cheese in the middle. When the cheese was melting and the bread was crispy, he plopped it onto a plate for me. It had a strange look and smell but I didn't have much else to eat.

"Thanks," I tried my best to sound grateful, though I might have been eying the sandwich like it was diseased. Goo was dripping out of the side when I picked it up. I nibbled of the corner. The bread wasn't awful. It was crunchy, even if it was still bland. The cheese was strange. I couldn't place the taste. It hadn't gone bad, but it didn't taste fresh, either. It was like he had taken it out of his emergency rations instead of going to the store and buying some more.

He stumbled off towards the shower. I fought my way through the meal, bit by bit. I hadn't struggled with eating something so much since I was a kid and refused certain vegetables. My dad would just sneak them into his cooking. This was a whole different level. It tasted weird. It felt greasy. The cheese was overpowering. After Delmar left, I took a knife and scraped most of the cheese off. It made the sandwich a lot easier to stomach.

I opted to drink some water and put a dab of the red liquid in for flavoring. It diluted the sweetness enough to be acceptable.

His pantry was nothing but emergency rations and I couldn't find where he kept his normal food. All I found were boxed or canned, preserved to last for a long time. Fruits, vegetables, soups... it was all canned. It was different from home, where we kept our rations in the basement. We didn't keep nearly as much, either. Rhodarens seemed to prepare themselves a lot more for a crisis.

"What did you do to my bathroom?" I heard him yell out from the other room. Both Deckard and I jumped to attention. If he wasn't injured, I imagined Delmar would have been running back to our room. Instead I heard the heavy thump of the cane banging on the ground as he rushed out.

"What do you mean?" I asked, confused.

"Someone hung up my towels everywhere!"

"Oh!" Comprehension dawned on me. "I was just trying to fix it."

"*Fix* it? Fix what?" he snapped at me.

"There's no wall between the shower and the toilet," I explained, frazzled.

"Yes there is."

"No, there's not!"

In an instant we were both rushing over to the bathroom to prove our points.

As soon as we got in the doorway I pointed at the shower and the toilet sitting next to it. "You see?"

"There's a glass wall right there," he retorted, pointing at the wall of the shower.

"But it's in the same room *right there*. It doesn't even reach the ceiling!" I answered, waving my arms at it.

"So what?"

"'So what?' You … you defecate there. How can you shower right next to it?"

He started ripping the towels down and piling them up. "There's nothing wrong with my shower."

"But it's right next to it. Do you want it to contaminate the place where you wash yourself?"

"It doesn't get in the shower. I'm perfectly clean."

I was stunned. Even the cheapest of places had the decency to separate them into different rooms, even if they were closely connected. "And what if someone needs to use the toilet while someone else is in the shower?"

"Then they can wait. I live here alone. It's not something I need to worry about," he growled at me, setting the pile of towels down on the counter. "Now stop messing up my things."

Frowning at him, I gave up and went back to the living room where Deckard was. How could he live like that? I couldn't imagine standing next to a toilet when I was trying to wash, but the stubborn man wouldn't listen. Why would they arrange a house like that?

I curled up on the couch. The food from earlier sat like a heavy weight in my stomach, but it was better than being empty. We had a break for a short while.

Delmar came back in some loose pajamas and prodded Deckard with the cane, making him move over so he could fall back onto the couch. Patting his lap, his lympet hobbled across the floor and jumped on it. Resting a hand around her, he pulled out the letters he'd taken from Breigah. Before we even had a chance to ask what he was doing, he began reading.

Dear Mom,

Things have been hectic lately with work and training. I don't seem to be picking it up as fast as I'd like, but I'm working really hard at it. If nothing else, at least I'll be able to fix it the next time our plumbing freezes.

Egrin bought some weird piece of junk again. We got into another argument. I keep telling him we don't have the money for it but he doesn't listen. If you're going to spend a thousand shills on a plate then it better poop gold as far as I'm concerned.

We're working things out, though. He said he won't do it again. It's not the first time he's said that, but I'm going to give him the benefit of the doubt. We're going on a short ice-fishing trip soon. At least I won't have to worry about him shopping while we're there.

How are things on the farm? I should come visit sometime with Lovel. I bet the weather is great right now. We don't get a lot of warm days up here.

Love, Ardus

Dear Mom,

The ice-fishing went great. Lovel caught one that weighed about half a pound. She was so excited. We caught five fish all together and cooked them up for dinner. It tasted great. Egrin is a good cook, if nothing else.

We went skating while we were out. Egrin is such a klutz on skates. It's amazing he didn't fall. He was flailing all over. I thought it was just a matter of time before I had to scrape him off the ice.

We really needed this break. Egrin is cute when he's trying to avoid smashing his face on the ground. We all had so much fun.

I'm glad everyone is getting their work done over there. At this point in your life, you should be taking it easy.

I always say it, but we need to visit sometime. It seems like we're never able to get there for some reason. We'll make it someday.

Love, Ardus

Dear Mom,

I'm so mad right now. Egrin spent three thousand shills on some pottery. THREE THOUSAND SHILLS. We had a huge fight about it. He has a serious addiction, I just can't deal with it anymore.

Every time he says he's got it out of his system, he goes back and does it again. I don't think he really cares about any of these things. And they just sit around the house collecting dust. He obsesses over them until he has them.

We seriously can't afford this, so I started selling the stuff while he's out. I'm not sure he'll even notice. He doesn't even look at them anymore, after he's had them a while. Hope things are going better over there.

Love, Ardus

It sounded like letters from the woman's daughter or son talking about everyday life. It didn't answer our questions about whom she was trying to kill or anything about the statue.

"Is that it?"

He flipped through the other letters. "It's all the same stuff. Not sure it really answers any questions." Tossing them on the table, he lifted himself to his feet. His leg trembled when he did. "Anyway, I'm going to hit the sack. We'll check out the place tomorrow." Scooping up Feenie, he headed back to his room.

Despite everything, the long days caught up to me, and I drifted off to sleep quickly.

17

5, 13, 3399
Liddenday

When I awoke, there was a stifling silence. I glanced over to see Deckard still lying on the other couch. I didn't want to wake him, and padded my way over to the window. A layer of snow blanketed the outside of the sill. Flakes continued floating down. Did the people here ever get a break?

Outside the window, the world moved on. The curtains partially covered me while I watched. A few people came out of their houses. I wondered where each was heading. What did they do? Living in Rhodaren was such a foreign concept. It felt so much different than Nagdecht.

It was only when the familiar truck pulled up to the front of the house that I realized Delmar had been missing. He came back through the door with a heavy limp and cane in one hand, and some fur coats in the other.

Seeing me awake, he tossed the coats on the couch Deckard was still lying on. "Here." Just as I took a step towards them he held out his hand, palm face-up with something in it. "Ah, and these things."

I changed my course for him. A pair of necklaces rested on his palm. I had no idea what to expect of Rhodaren jewelry.

One had a round sapphire in the middle with wavy silver flowing out of it, like a blue sun. The bottom portion dipped further down, while the sides had symmetrical curved designs that led up to another smaller, but similar, set of blue suns on either side.

The second looked more like the design of an abstract flower with thorns on the petals. Instead of a stamen, it had a black onyx.

The closer I looked at them, the more I saw that they were fashioned smoothly and with purpose. The craftsmanship was excellent, and had a different feel than the Naggian jewelry that usually replicated nature in design.

I smiled. "Valli will love these."

"Who's Valli?" Deckard asked from behind me.

I swung my head around, surprised to see him awake. "He's a friend at home. He's into foreign stuff. These will be perfect when his birthday comes up." They were packed into my bag before I could forget them. In light of the recent death, the conversation felt weird. It didn't feel like we should be sitting around casually talking, but I didn't know what to do about it.

I picked up one of the coats he had thrown down. It had a leather exterior while the interior was lined with soft fur. They had hats to go with them, as well as gloves and some other piece of cloth I couldn't identify. I picked it up. "What's this?"

"You can wrap that around your mouth, like how the soldiers do."

His explanation only helped a little because our soldiers didn't wrap anything around their mouths. "I thought Rhodaren soldiers had uniforms that looked like Geuranians', except black."

"They're similar. But ours are built to withstand the weather. High collars are a normal part of the uniform. But I had to buy those separate."

I hadn't seen a Rhodaren soldier, so I didn't have a great picture of it. I held the cloth up to my mouth.

"I figure it'll help you guys cover up, too. So people won't notice you."

I looked at the full outfit. It did cover a lot. With our heads and mouths covered, only the space around our eyes would be showing. We were a lot less likely to be spotted as long as we didn't get too close to people. The coat was too big on me, but I was fine with that.

"I bought one for a teenager, but even they're not that small," Delmar told me. I was a little small. Standing next to my dad always reminded me of that, even though I'd finally reached 6'6". But he was tall and muscular, so I looked tiny in comparison.

The Rhodarens had an entirely different level of what was an acceptable size, though. I could've fit both of my arms in one sleeve. Since that meant more coat to keep me warm, I didn't mind.

I pulled on the hat and wrapped the cover around my mouth. With it all on inside of the house, I was hot. It was a welcome relief when I knew it would only last a short time.

Deckard chuckled and I glanced at him.

"You look like a kid wearing his dad's clothes."

I raised a brow at him. "I'd like to see you try these on."

He pulled on the other one. His fit slightly better, but it was still loose.

"Are you two ready to go to the house then?"

I dreaded going to her house. At the same time, it was the first place we could think to look that made sense. We might find a lead there to discover who Holf was, and where she put the statue. I swallowed my unease and nodded.

It wasn't a long drive from his place to the house where he'd met her. It was my first time getting to look at the place, and for once we were walking around Rhodaren in the daytime.

It looked like an old, wooden cabin. The floor creaked when we walked inside. The first room didn't have too much in it. A piano sat in the corner of the room with a music book on it, and there was a table with a knife sticking out of it. Delmar limped over to the table and we were quick behind him.

The knife pinned a picture of a woman to the table. She was smiling, but the face of the other person in the photo had been stabbed repeatedly. I couldn't even tell if it was a man or a woman. The woman looked to be in her thirties, maybe.

"I guess we won't get much from that. Maybe it's her daughter?" I said. Behind me, Deckard continued into the next room. I slowly wandered around the room, scanning it all over, until I came to the piano.

I studied the booklet sitting on it. It was turned to some kind of waltz, but I wasn't much of a musician.

Deckard returned and lingered in front of the door frame. At first I didn't pay much attention, but something about his posture seemed odd. When I looked at him, he had an arm wrapped around his stomach and looked confused.

"Don't go in there," he said, but it sounded more like an invitation to go in.

I took a step closer and he didn't stop me. Our eyes met as I walked by. It was a hallway that had a few doors, but only one was ajar. Without any lights on and no windows in the hallway, I went through the darkness to the next room.

It was a bedroom with a large window. One bed was in the middle with brown sheets, little dressers on both sides and a chair in the corner. But the alarming part was the blood.

Somehow I missed it at first, but when I turned, I saw blood spatter covering the wall. I jumped back. The spatter went all the way to the door frame where I was standing. My eyes scanned the room again, looking for more traces. There were a couple small streaks of blood on the wall, as if rubbed there. And then there was a large red spot on the floor.

When I looked back, Deckard had followed me. I fled from the room back to the front. Delmar was sitting on the piano bench with the cane by his side.

"Someone was murdered in there," I said.

"Oh?"

"This wasn't Breigah's house, right? Do you know whose it was?"

"How did you know that?" Delmar asked.

"Overheard it."

He glared at me, but continued, "Probably her daughter's house."

"You think maybe the husband killed her and ran off?" Deckard asked.

A silence fell over us for a moment before Delmar broke it. "I've been thinking. Take a look at this place."

I glanced around. I didn't see anything in particular in this room.

"Doesn't it seem awfully empty considering people lived here? I mean, there's furniture here, but where are all the decorations?"

He was right. The house looked bare.

"The letters said that he was buying a bunch of expensive things, right? Maybe that attracted a burglar. Besides, she was after Holf, and the husband's name was Egrin."

"So you think she tried to lure out the burglar and kill him?"

"Maybe. What do the other rooms look like?"

I was hesitant to check, but Deckard went with me. There wasn't any blood in the other rooms, but they did lack common décor. Furniture was in the building, but nothing that was mentioned in the letters. No plates, or pottery, or anything else unique. Delmar may have been right. They could have been robbed.

There was another bedroom that just had a few pieces of furniture in it, and typical rooms.

We headed back to the first room.

"There's no more blood, but the rest of the house is kind of bare, too."

"Then we're probably looking for a burglar."

"So Holf was probably his name. Can we find him based on that?"

"We can look around, sure, but it would help if we knew what area he lived in."

"Wouldn't he probably live around here?"

"It's possible. He might also be someone who made deals with the husband. I can look into it."

"How do you guys find information like this? I tried to look it up on the access panels, but I couldn't find anything."

"The access panels? What were you looking there for?" He gave me an odd look.

"Where else would I look? Shouldn't they have everyone's information?"

When he spoke, he sounded like he thought that was a bizarre idea, "People don't want just anyone to be able to look up where they live. What if they have a stalker or something?"

"You could block the stalker from being able to look them up?"

"How would you be able to tell that they were the ones looking?"

"Using their IDs."

"Access panels don't take IDs."

I paused. I hadn't thought much about it, but they didn't. They hadn't in Geuran, either. Which had been fortunate for me since I didn't have an ID for either country. It did make it confusing to figure out how they shared their information and got around.

"All right, then, what about news? How do you guys get news?" I questioned further.

151

"You could keep up with the reports if you want to sit around and stare at video, but the best way is to get a copy of the local news when you're in an area."

"The ... local news? How do you do that?"

"You can pick one up at a store."

"'One'? One what?" I asked, trying to imagine what he was buying.

"It's like a booklet. Reporters find the stories and print them all up."

"Wait, it's not run by the government?"

He gave me another odd look. "Of course not. Free press here."

"But how do you know you can trust the stories if they're not being regulated?" More and more Rhodaren was looking like a wild, out of control country. How did they manage to keep anything regulated?

"Some sources are more reliable than others, but the real question is how can you trust the news if the government is the one deciding what you hear?" He pointed at me.

"What ...?" I stared in shock for a moment. No one had ever challenged me on the issue. When something was reported in Nagdecht, the information had to be verified. Errors rarely got through. I placed my hands on my hips and defended our system, "Our news reports have to be proven to be legitimate before they're reported. Our information is extremely reliable!"

"How can you be sure of that? You think they're always telling you the truth?" he sounded skeptical.

"Why would they lie? Making sure people have correct information benefits us all!"

In my whole life, I never had a reason to question the validity of our news and information.

Then I met General Glaive. I knew he used misinformation as a weapon. He even went as far as making a false report that he'd been shot. The report was later retracted and explained as an error countrywide, but I knew it was intentional. I also knew he had reasons for doing it, but it still planted a kernel of doubt in me. How often did that happen?

"Can you prove what they tell you is true?" he asked.

"Well, I personally can't … but how can you prove any of the news you read is true, either? You said yourself some are more reliable than others, which means a lot of them are wrong," I challenged him. I still had faith in our system, even if it had been tarnished a little.

"I know that. Reading multiple versions of the same story is the best way to get to the truth. That's why our news is the best. We have all sorts of sources to turn to. If one book doesn't cover it, another will."

"Well, then …" I sputtered, flustered. "If it's so great, then let's see what it tells us about all this!" I waved at the floor and the house. A murder certainly deserved to be reported.

"That I will." He pushed up to his feet. "I can go get some reports right now."

That caused me to nearly lunge after him when he took a step towards the door. "Wait!"

He looked back at me, and I flushed at my over-reaction, calming. "I don't want to stay here." I waved my arms towards the hallway. "In the murder house!"

"You're going to be a handful, aren't you?"

"That's what I think," Deckard finally butted in to make a joke. The whole time we had argued, he had remained silent and out of the way. I gave him a pointed look, but he just smirked at me.

"What if something happens?" I asked.

153

"I've got my phone on me. Do you have anything?"

I reached into my pocket and pulled the little thing out. Saying that it was 'mine' was a rather loose interpretation of the facts.

"This thing? Yeah, even though it's outdated."

"What are you talking about?"

"I mean, don't you guys even have v-phones yet here?"

"V-phones?"

"You know. With video?"

"Why would I want to see video when I'm talking to someone?"

"Why *wouldn't* you want to see video?"

"What if I need to take a dump?"

I gaped at him. "Why would you talk on the phone while you're doing *that*?"

"Because sometimes it's convenient."

"That's gross. But I still don't want to stay here. What if police come to investigate more? Or what if someone other than Breigah comes to take a look?"

Delmar let out a heavy sigh. "All right. I'll drive you back to my place first."

We packed back into the front of the truck. Deckard stayed in the middle since he knew how to drive in case of an emergency, and I sat by the passenger window. I was quickly learning to appreciate having a Rhodaren with us. Driving around was much more convenient and comfortable than walking.

I pulled my new coat around myself. "At least this coat keeps me a bit warm."

"If you weren't such a stick you wouldn't get cold so fast."

"There's nothing wrong with how big I am," I snapped. "You don't have to try and make fun of me."

"Oh, please. I've traveled around, I know how you guys talk about us. You make fun of how big we are, our noses, our ears, our government ..."

Fat, big noses, weird curved ears, do-nothing government ... I felt ashamed I could come up with so much. I'd never thought deeply on the subject before. When did I pick up all these ideas?

"Well, you can't say that like you guys don't talk about us!" I snapped back.

Deckard held his head, groaning between us. "Why am I in the middle?" He looked to me. "Do you want to switch places?"

"I don't know how to drive. What if something happens?"

"I'm willing to take that risk," he said.

"I'm not switching seats," I told him.

I folded my arms and sat firmly in place until we got to the house to wait.

He came back later with some food and a pile of booklets. The paper in them was thin. Some were thick and covered a wide range of subjects. Others were around twenty pages and only covered current local news. Each one had an index in the front, dividing the stories by type and giving a short title for each article. It seemed like a slow, clunky way of looking up information.

We sat down and started sorting through them as a group, looking through the local stories. In one of the larger papers, he found a short article about a murder in the area. I found a similar story in one of the little books. We set them on the table and compared them.

A woman was beaten to death, and her husband and daughter were missing. The articles speculated about different theories. One suggested the husband might be the culprit. The other suspected it was a home invasion. They didn't seem to know much

155

more about it than we did, except we now knew she had been married with a child, and two people were missing.

So the Rhodaren woman had a daughter named Ardus, a granddaughter named Lovel, and a son-in-law named Egrin. It didn't have their address or anything, but we already knew where the house was.

"So what do you think happened to the husband and granddaughter? No one has found them yet," I said.

"It's possible they were taken hostage or killed elsewhere. There's no way of knowing yet. It seems like she thought Holf was the culprit, so we should probably look for him right now."

"Where did you guys meet him?" Deckard piped in.

"A bar in Hulsben. He probably lives somewhere around there."

"Then how about we start there?" I said.

18
5, 13, 3399
Liddenday

Music assaulted our ears on the drive to Hulsben. While I didn't mind listening to new songs, they sounded as if they hadn't been properly fixed up, and on top of that, Delmar was singing loudly along with it. His voice wasn't bad, but it was awkward listening to him sing without a care. It was like he thought he was alone in the washroom.

During the drive, Deckard leaned towards me and whispered in my ear, "I can see why she left him behind."

I cracked a small smile. It didn't feel appropriate, but it still felt nice to talk like normal. Delmar's eyes flicked our way, but he didn't say anything.

Finally, with a frustrated sigh, I asked him, "Don't you have something better to listen to?"

"What are you talking about? This is a good song."

"It's not that bad, but it hasn't been tuned right or something." My lack of music jargon showed.

"Tuned? It's fine."

"The singer is okay, but she's not hitting everything perfectly. They should have fixed the song before airing it."

He let out a disagreeable grunt. "You either have the talent or you don't. I don't want to listen to some computer sing."

For a moment, I was stunned. My initial thought had been that maybe Rhodarens didn't have the technology to adjust music. They were behind on so many other things that it would make sense. He didn't seem confused by my suggestion at all, though. It sounded more like he just wasn't interested.

"But it's off a bit in some spots."

"That's just part of what makes the song unique."

I stopped arguing with him. It was an unusual perspective he had, and after pondering on it, I realized it must have been a common perspective among Rhodarens if they were leaving their music like that. It was different. It sounded ... old. Leaning to the side as I listened, I gazed out the window.

The world passed by outside. Some kids were playing in the snow. A lympet was with them, jumping around. They piled the snow into different shapes and pulled sleds behind them.

"What bar did you guys find him in?" I asked.

"It's one in the middle of town."

"Maybe we can ask if he's a regular there. Then we'd know if he lives or works nearby, at least."

"And we might spot him," Deckard added.

"Here's the plan: I'll go in and ask some questions. You guys sit in the truck and keep an eye on the place. If he's a frequent customer, we can wait for him to show up and follow him home."

"Wait, we don't know what he looks like," I reminded him.

"Then you two can lay low. If he shows up, I'll come out and we can follow him."

"Isn't he going to notice if a truck is following him?"

"We'll figure something out. Let's go."

He parked us outside of a bar and left Deckard and me in the truck. We covered ourselves up while we waited.

It was a long night. I was thankful when darkness fell and obscured us even more. Eventually

Delmar came back out. He had a bag with him, and handed us some crackers. If nothing else, they weren't difficult to eat. We split them and munched away.

"The barkeep said that he comes here sometimes, but he didn't come tonight."

"We can't just sit here night after night waiting for him. Isn't there some other way we can find him?"

"Let me think," he said, taking a moment. "Someone here might know about him. I can always ask around."

He went back into the bar.

At first, I wanted to keep a diligent watch, but as time went on I got weary of staring out the window. I wouldn't even know who to look for anyway. I glanced at Deckard. His head was turned away from me, staring at something in the distance. Or perhaps he wasn't paying attention to where he was looking and he was just thinking. Here we had this time together, and we hadn't really talked much at all. We were so caught up in everything that was happening.

"Deckard?"

"Hmm?" His gaze swung back to me.

"What do you think of Delmar?"

"I don't know." He shrugged. "He's a Rhodaren."

"He kind of weird." I crossed my arms.

"You're kind of weird." He smirked at me with a quirked brow.

"I am not!" I whined at him. My response was too genuine for my own tastes. I didn't mean to feel offended but since we were all together I was feeling more and more out of place. Fortunately, he didn't take my answer seriously and went back to looking out the window. It gave me a moment to recover. "You haven't been talking much lately."

His gaze flicked my way for half a second. His voice was strained, "I just don't want to get stuck in the middle of anything."

My ears sunk and I stared at the floor of the truck. "Sorry. It's just … Don't you think he does a lot of stuff weird? Like having a toilet next to the shower."

"I've seen worse."

"You have?"

He grinned at me. "I saw a toilet in the kitchen once."

I flinched. "Why would anyone put it there?"

He shrugged. I fidgeted with my fingers.

About twenty minutes passed before Delmar came back out. He hopped into the driver's side again. "All right, I have a location."

I was stunned. I didn't expect so much. "Really?"

"There was someone else there who's dealt with him before. Seemed a little upset with him, so I just said I was having problems with him, too. Anyway, I know the basic area where he's living. What do you want to do?"

"Basic idea? How basic?" I asked.

"I know what neighborhood he lives in."

"Then trying to find him during the night is probably a bad idea. We don't know which house to go to. Let's try again in the morning."

The decision was made. We had trouble finding a place where we could sleep without Deckard and me being noticed, but we found a small inn with rooms detached from the main building. Delmar rented a room for the night, and we crept in. We curled up in a spot out of view of the window and door and got some sleep.

Early in the morning, we drove to the neighborhood and parked by the side of the street where a man was out for a stroll.

"Wait here a moment," Delmar told us, as he hopped out of the truck. He trotted after the man and whistled at him. "Hey, where are you going, hot stuff?"

The man paused, glancing back at him with an amused look before responding flatly, "I'm engaged."

"That can always be fixed," Delmar teased.

Turning around and placing a hand on his hip, the man looked as if he was trying to emulate exasperation, but he was too amused for it to come off as genuine.

"All right smooth talker. What do you want?"

"You're from around here. Happen to know where a guy named Holf lives?"

"Don't know him."

"He's a bit of a traveler. He probably would have been using a snowmobile lately."

"Someone has been driving a snowmobile here lately …"

"Great! Any idea which direction he goes?"

The man held his hand in front of his mouth, glancing behind him before answering. "I believe it's left down that street and go something like five streets down. There should be a bunch of little streets in there. They're all named after birds," he explained.

"Thanks muchly," Delmar answered with a hasty salute before bounding back to the vehicle. The other man continued on his way – but I caught him glancing back with a smile.

The more time I spent in the country, the more I slowly became accustomed to how they looked. I tried to see why other Rhodarens would find him attractive. His hair was all right, with thick curls. The rest still didn't make much sense to me.

Rhodarens were so opposite of what we considered attractive in Nagdecht that they were the epitome of what not to do. I had never even questioned it. "Handsome" and "Rhodaren" simply didn't belong in the same sentence.

We crawled down the streets until we spotted a snowmobile parked in front of one of the houses.

"That's the place?" I asked.

"It could be. Snowmobiles aren't all that uncommon, but most people don't need them every day," he explained. He pulled farther down the street, so the truck would be less noticeable, and we played the waiting game.

After about two hours, a man came out of the house. It was my first time seeing him. From a distance, I could see he had a brown jacket with fur lining, and hair tied behind his back.

Delmar didn't wait. He hopped out of the truck, limping a few steps forward.

"Hey!" he called out.

The man looked in our direction, jumped back, then fled the other way.

"Hey!" he yelled again. He took one quick step after the man before realizing his folly and heading back for the truck. He started it up and pulled out, spinning the truck around to follow him. The man ran to the nearest boarding spot for carts, and before we could catch him, he sped away.

"We lost him again," I grumbled.

"But we know where his home is," Delmar reminded me.

Home invasion was something new for me, but the man had information somewhere. He was the only clue we had in figuring out why Breigah had tried to murder him and where she had put the statue. There was also a good chance he was a burglar himself, so in a way, he probably deserved it.

"Think we can do it without getting noticed?"

"If we hurry up. No one is really out yet. I'll park the truck in front to block the view, come on."

He parked the truck in front of the door. We hopped out, and I picked the lock. Knowing it was empty and we needed to get inside to avoid being spotted got me to work fast. We rushed inside and shut the door behind us.

"You don't think he'll call the police, do you?" Deckard asked.

"I doubt it. I know he killed a woman. He probably doesn't want to explain that to them."

It was a small home. I walked inside to get an overview of the layout, glancing around.

A small thump caught my ear. I barely had time to take in my surroundings. Muffled footsteps ran down the hallway away from us.

"Someone's in here!" I whispered to the others.

I dashed to the hallway. The sound went to the left, into one of the rooms. I sprinted down the hall. Grabbing the door frame, I swung around into the room.

I didn't see anyone immediately. The other two stepped in behind me, keeping a wary eye out. My eyes darted everywhere. My body tensed. I was ready for an attack.

When I inched around the bed I saw a small body curled up behind it. She was a young girl. Her head was tucked against her knees and she covered it, shivering. We exchanged looks. I wanted comfort her, but being Naggian I would probably just scare her if I got any closer.

"Ah …" I was at a loss for words. "Don't worry, we're not here to hurt you."

She curled up even tighter.

"We're just … uh …" I looked to the other two for help. "We were just here to find something. That's all." I waved them over, not wanting to be the only one trying to fix things, and whispered harshly at them, "Come on!"

"I should stay back here," Deckard replied. He was right. If there was one thing that would scare Rhodaren more than a Naggian, it was a Geuranian. He disappeared into the hallway.

"I'm not really a kid person," Delmar responded with his hands stuffed in his jacket pockets.

I tugged on him. "Come on, let her pet your lympet or something."

He wrapped his arms protectively around the bag and spat back, "She can get her own lympet!"

"Just let her!"

He inched closer, a frown on his face as he took a seat by the girl and reluctantly held the bag between them. Feenie's head was sticking out of it. The girl peeked out from her knees. A hand hesitantly reached out, touching the fur on the lympet's head. Like always, Feenie did little more than slightly acknowledge her existence. She ran her hand over it, brushing down the fur from her head to the bag.

"Not so hard," Delmar grumbled. He lifted her closer to himself, petting her gently.

With her calming down, I tried to explain again, "No one is going to hurt you. We just needed to look around. Nothing bad is going to happen."

She stayed quiet. I couldn't tell if she believed me or not.

"What should we do?" I asked him. I hadn't planned on anyone being inside. "Are you sure we got the right place?"

"This should be Holf's place. It's possible Breigah was wrong about who she was looking for," Delmar answered.

The girl perked up. "You know Grandma?"

Silence descended upon us. Things just got a million times worse. Breigah was dead, and this girl had no idea. Not to mention that meant her mother was also dead, and the status of her father was uncertain. Had she been kidnapped? Why was she with Holf?

"Uh … Yeah, we know her. We were traveling with her and she wanted us to do some stuff for her," I tried to explain.

"Where is she?"

I flinched at the question.

"She …" I tried to think of an answer.

"She wasn't able to make it, so we came here for her," Delmar answered in my place.

"Do you know Holf?" I asked.

She quieted again, staring down at the floor. I noticed the bright yellow beaded bracelet on her wrist when her hair fell over her knees. It seemed to contrast sharply with her mood.

"Nevermind. Give us a minute, okay?" I tried to take the pressure off her and backed out of the room, gesturing for the other two to join me. We gathered in the next room and whispered.

"What should we do? It looks like she was kidnapped. We can't leave her here," I said.

"We can't very well call the police while we're here," Deckard replied.

"I can call them after we leave and report it," Delmar answered.

"Then we have to make sure we look at everything we want to look at right now," I said.

We started searching for the documents and any other information we could find. I realized that it would probably scare the girl again, so I went back to the room. She was peeking over the side of the bed. I sat down on the edge. As much as I wanted to look non-threatening, it had never been a problem before in my life so I didn't know what to do.

I could at least keep her calm while the other two were searching. "So, hey … You must be Lovel?"

"Yeah."

"I bet you've never met a Naggian before, right?" I started. Maybe if I pointed out the obvious, I could make light of it.

"A what …?"

"Umm, I think people say 'Nadder' here. But I don't really like that. We're Naggians," I explained.

"Oh." She shook her head.

"Well … Do you have any questions about Nagdecht?"

"Isn't Nagdecht supposed to be really far away?"

"Ah, heh, yeah, it is. There's Geuran, Lyruna or that frozen tundra up above between us."

"Then how did you get here?"

"I hitched a ride in Geuran." I glanced towards the hall. "Deckard … I know he's a Geuranian, but he's not really scary at all."

She started coming out of her hiding spot, standing on the other side of the bed. It was difficult for me to determine her age. I'd never seen a Rhodaren child before, and they looked a lot different than Naggians. Based on her height, I guessed around ten, possibly under. Her figure was heavyset, with thick, long, and curly hair. Rhodarens seemed to be fond of long hair. Her ears curved back and her large nose had a slight bump in the middle.

"How do you know Grandma?"

"We … We all happened to be looking for the same thing, and I guess you could say we bumped into each other. I'm pretty sure she wanted to see you, too, but … she just wasn't able to make it," I explained. I wasn't at all prepared to inform her about the old woman's death.

"Where is she?"

"She's … It's hard to explain. But I'm sure she'd be here if she could."

166

I wasn't sure what to bring up. I didn't want to bring up her parents. I didn't know if she knew her mother was dead, or if she even witnessed it. But there was still one question.

"Do you know where your dad is?" I asked gently.

She looked down at her hands, shrugging a little. I hoped he wasn't dead, too, for her sake.

When I caught myself frowning I forced myself to flash a smile again, wanting to keep her calm. "I see. Don't worry, we'll make sure that the police come here. I'm going to check on the other two."

I left the room. Deckard and Delmar were browsing through the house, opening drawers, cabinets, and everything that might have the documents.

"Anything?" I asked.

"Nothing yet. Just some ID, which doesn't help much when we already know who he is."

"Maybe he took it with him," I suggested.

"It's possible. He was leaving, so he might have been going somewhere with it. Maybe she wrote down something about where she put it." Delmar shrugged.

"Maybe we should figure out how to find him instead. Any ideas on how to catch up to him?"

"Just one. If we can figure out how to connect to his phone from here, then we might be able to use that."

"I don't know. He'll probably guess it's us if we try calling him."

"I don't have anything else."

I sighed. "All right, see if you can find his number. Maybe we can figure out something to do with it."

The number was easy enough to find when we looked on the desk where his home phone was. We wrote it down and put it with our stuff.

I went back to the girl's room. We still needed to resolve things with her.

"Hey, we're going to head out, but we'll make sure the police come here soon. You probably shouldn't tell them that a Naggian and Geuranian are around. Okay?"

She furrowed her brows, but nodded at me.

"Promise?" I pleaded.

She nodded again.

"All right. Just wait here, then. The police will be here soon."

I started to head out when she called after me, "Umm …"

I glanced back.

"Can you tell Grandma to come get me?"

A knife went through my heart. I did my best to hold myself together. "I … will if I see her."

Deckard and I shuffled outside and Delmar waved us into the back of the truck. We didn't argue. The more hidden we were at the moment, the better.

He called up the police and let them know the girl was there, and that she was the daughter of a murdered woman from the other town. We waited to make sure no one got there before the police, then we drove off.

Now, it was a matter finding out where the man was going. Delmar pulled outside of town so that we could move around freely without worrying about getting caught. We got out of the truck to stretch, and Delmar set his lympet down on the ground.

"He's looking for the statue. So maybe it's a matter of figuring out the most likely place to find it."

"If you think about it, she had a limited amount of time to hide it, right?" Deckard said.

"You're right." I looked at Delmar. "Because she was with you."

"All I know about is the box."

"She didn't take anything else new with her?"

"Not that I saw."

"So it has to be back near that greenhouse place somewhere."

"All right then. You want to drive all the way back there?"

"Yeah. And ... food," I said. My stomach growled.

"No problem. I have some stuff from home."

We dug a pit and started up a fire. He hung a small cauldron over it. I was hoping for soup again. It had been decent compared to the other things I had tasted.

Instead, he filled it with a cheesy looking substance. He took out a bag full of biscuits and passed them out. I wasn't sure what to do with it, but he tore pieces off of his and pierced it on the end of a large fork, dipping it into the cheesy sauce and taking a bite.

The bread was hard in my hands when I squeezed it.

"This bread is hard," I told him.

"Yeah. We need to eat it before it goes bad."

I stared at him. "But it already *is* bad. It's stale!"

"It's fine," he answered.

Tearing a piece off, I glared at it. It wasn't like we had much else to eat. The cheese had a thin layer near the sides that had hardened and wrinkled when pushed. Steam came off of the bread when I pulled it out, but it quickly cooled. I popped it in my mouth. It was warm, and a little better than the cheese I'd eaten the other day, but it still felt strange and heavy.

"Well, it's warm," I said in a poor attempt at being positive.

Deckard gave a laugh. He seemed to handle it better than I, but I didn't know much about Geuranian standards of food. "Definitely warms up the stomach," he said.

169

Delmar pulled out a bottle. It didn't have any labels on it, and looked like something he carried and filled up for himself.

"If you want to warm up, this will do the trick, too."

He drank some, and passed the bottle to Deckard, who took a quick swig before passing it to me. I was so thirsty I didn't even ask what it was, throwing my head back to down it, expecting some sort of juice. It took a moment for a burning sensation to register in my throat, and I yanked the bottle away. The last trickled down and the sensation subsided, leaving me in shock. I'd never had anything like it before.

"How much alcohol is in this?" I asked in a panic.

"I don't know. Forty, fifty percent?" Delmar shrugged.

"Forty ... Don't you people have any standards?" I yelled.

"What are you talking about?" he asked. The more we talked, the less patience he seemed to have with me.

I coughed, throat feeling itchy after I'd reacted in a panic. "It shouldn't be above ten percent!"

"Says who?"

"It's the law!"

"Not here, it isn't."

I fanned my face as it began heating up. My heart was racing. I felt lightheaded. I dropped the drink on the ground and wandered away from them, for once thankful for the snow as flakes landed on my face. I had no idea how much I'd drunk, and it scared me how much my body was already reacting. I'd never felt my heart pound like this when I wasn't exercising, and the anxiety only made it worse.

"What's wrong?" Deckard asked.

"I don't feel so good."

"Are all Nadders such lightweights?" Delmar asked. He relaxed, staying in his spot, completely unconcerned about me. "To think we were actually worried about you guys. All we'd have to do to win a war with you is invite you for some drinks and leave you out in the cold."

When I looked back, he had picked up the bottle and was taking another drink from it, while I was terrified. I didn't like feeling my heart beating so sporadically. My hand clung to my chest as if to hold it back. I leaned against the tree with my eyes on the ground. Nausea welled up in my stomach and I wondered if I should vomit. I hated the thought of throwing up, but the thought of getting what I could out of my system was tempting.

A hand patted my back and I glanced behind me.

"Just sit down for a while. It'll wear off," Deckard said.

Panting, I dragged myself back to the fire and sat down. A lump sat at the bottom of my stomach.

"Eat something. It'll slow the alcohol down," Delmar suggested.

The pot of weird cheese taunted me. I didn't want to stomach it at the moment, but if he was right, then it was the only thing around to eat. I needed to get more into my stomach, anyway. Cheese hung off the piece of bread when I dipped it in. The flavor was overpowering. The next bite, I only dipped partially in and slowly ate my way through the old biscuit. With every bite, I felt the lump growing.

I wrapped up in my coat. Deckard seemed to be okay with the food and alcohol. Delmar looked downright delighted with it. I couldn't remember ever eating bread after it had gotten hard before. We always had it fresh. Almost all of our food was like that. When we made something we ate it within a day or two. If something like bread went stale, we composted it. Delmar seemed to keep things wrapped up and sitting around.

"Any ideas where she could have gone when you weren't with her?" Deckard asked him.

"She couldn't have gone far. I always had the truck, and she wasn't any sort of runner." He wiped his mouth with his sleeve, still eating the fondue. "At least, not for the most part."

"So she had to hide it close to that greenhouse. What about that other woman who was staying there?"

"I don't know. She turned us away when I was there."

"Really?" I was surprised. She had shooed Deckard and me away, but I hadn't suspected she acted the same towards other Rhodarens. "She told us that she gave it to you guys."

Delmar furrowed his eyebrows. "You talked to her?"

"Yeah."

"Strange. She didn't call anyone."

I butted in, "Maybe she doesn't have a means of communication out there." I glanced at Deckard. "And we may have taken her method of transportation."

"Very strange. But I guess if she's trapped, she's trapped."

"Do you think she'd be okay out there alone?" I asked him. If she had no method of contact and no transportation, it could be hard for her to get food or water.

"If she lives out there, I'm sure she knows how to last a while. But she's probably going to run into problems without any vehicles for too long."

I looked at Deckard. "I guess we should make sure to get that snowmobile thing back to her."

"Fine with me." He shrugged. "We're headed that way anyhow."

"I wonder why she would have given Breigah the statue if she turned you guys away when you were there," I pondered aloud.

"Well, she did have a gun. I never saw it until the other day, so maybe when I was gone Granny threatened her," Delmar suggested.

"So, we'll bring the vehicle back for her, and check all around the greenhouse for the statue," I went over the plan.

We agreed and hopped back into the truck to make the trip back. Our journey was only disturbed by the frequent bathroom breaks Delmar took. It slowed down our progress a lot. It was no wonder we were able to catch up to the two before. Just outside of the mountain town, we stopped for a break and so Delmar could pick up extra supplies. I spent most of the time holding myself and leaning against the side of the truck while my stomach protested.

We put blankets in the back of the truck and set it up.

"All right, we're all set for the night," he said.

"We need something to eat, too," I reminded him. Deckard gave a small grunt of agreement.

"No problem. I can make some more fondue," he said.

I didn't want to directly insult his dish, but my stomach was yelling every insult in the book. "Actually ... I was thinking maybe getting clam chowder or something?" I suggested.

He let out a loud laugh, settling into a chuckle before he looked over at me staring at him.

"Oh, you're serious," he said in disbelief.

"Of course I'm serious. Why wouldn't I be serious?" I retorted.

He stepped closer to me, grabbing my shoulders and spinning me around to face the woods.

"Take a look, Nadder. Do you see any clams?"

It was nothing but a blanket of snow with evil trees.

"No, but ..."

"*This* is what we've got. Almost the entire country is covered in snow. Half of our land is permanently frozen. We've barely got any good farmlands, and these guys," he pointed at Deckard with his thumb, "keep trying to take it."

My eyes turned to Deckard. I sighed and dropped my shoulders, mumbling, "Yeah, they cause us problems, too."

"Hey." Deckard placed his hands on his hips, quirking a brow. "Don't look at me. I didn't do anything. You've said yourself, I'm lousy at my job."

"I know, but your people are still way too violent," I said.

"Give me a break. It's not even like I'm into our government." He shrugged and turned away.

"This is what we've got," Delmar continued firmly. "We spend half the time just battling off famines. Hell, there was a huge one about fifteen years ago."

Something clicked in my mind. Fifteen years ago?

"A famine?" I repeated as I worked it out in my mind. "Was it a disease that was killing the crops?"

"Yeah," he answered. His tone softened as he became more curious than irritated.

I pointed towards myself energetically. "We had that, too! In the northern part of Nagdecht, a ton of the crops were diseased."

The strange, morbid connection struck me. Somehow I had never even considered the possibility that the disease had spread so wide because it didn't affect us. In my mind I had always imagined the disease affected the northern part of Nagdecht and that was it. I had never thought it had hit the entirety of the northern part of the continent, including Rhodaren.

"What did you guys do?" I asked.

He shook his head. "We tried to cut around the diseased parts and use the rest of the crops."

My eyes widened. "But you have to burn them or people could get sick!"

"People did get sick," he answered bluntly.

"See?"

"It was either that or starve," he said matter-of-factly. "We don't have thousands of miles of extra land. We can't just go grab food from somewhere else. There is no other food."

I frowned. "What happened?"

"What do you mean?"

"I mean, you said people got sick. We destroyed all of the infected crops so no one got sick. What happened to them?"

"They drowned, essentially."

"Drowned?" I drew my brows together.

"It messed up their lungs. Basically, you could say it punched holes in their lungs, and bodily fluids would start to get into them. It took a long time to be fatal, though," he explained.

Wincing, I tried to keep myself from imagining it. "That's an awful way to go."

"Well, we're not as lucky as you guys. We don't have massive amounts of land for food."

I pursed my lips. "We had it hard, too. The whole northern part of the country was out of food. We tried to get food to everyone, but it was millions of people. Some of the weaker people didn't make it."

"The kids and the elderly?"

I shook my head. "The elderly. If people had food around, they fed the kids first." I shrugged. "That's just how it works."

He stayed silent for a moment before shaking his head and walked to the other side of the fire. "Doesn't sound much more fun than drowning."

"Yeah ..."

We settled down around the fire, and he started a fondue. I gave up on the idea of having something more. The heat of the fire and food wafted around, giving us a little warmth. It was the first time I really felt attached to Rhodarens in some way.

"I guess the Geuranians didn't have to deal with any of that," Delmar said, bringing Deckard into the conversation.

"We didn't have a famine, but the Naggians did attack us." His eyes turned to me and I looked back uncomfortably. Delmar leaned forward, arm over his knee, his other hand around his lympet.

"They did?"

"Yeah," Deckard's gaze turned to him, "they attacked a bunch of our little villages on the border. There's mountains near there, but before you actually hit the boundary, there's a bunch of flatlands, and a lot of rural places out there. They killed a bunch of our farmers before they got to Clearwater."

The conversation started out grim, but at the very end, Deckard grinned.

"A military camp?" Delmar asked.

"A tiny fishing and farming village on the mountainside," Deckard corrected him happily. "They had three rifles in the whole place and they held the army off for seven days."

"How did they manage that?" Delmar seemed stunned.

"They burned their crops, built up walls, rolled rocks down the hills," Deckard began listing the ways enthusiastically. "Two of the people were wesp farmers. They smoked the wesps, collected them into jars while they were unconscious, and they made a makeshift slingshot to launch them into the soldiers."

I couldn't share Deckard's enthusiasm knowing that Naggians were on the receiving end of that. I could only imagine how painful it would be to be swarmed by wesps.

"You sound pretty excited about that," I said hesitantly.

"Because they're awesome. Just imagine a little farm village fighting off an entire army!" He laughed.

"That is unbelievable," Delmar replied.

I had no idea Deckard was into anything like that. He didn't usually seem to care much for fighting or politics, but watching him talk to Delmar about fighting us off made me feel left out. The Geuranians were scared of us. The Rhodarens didn't care for us, either. How did we become the big bad guy? We were peaceful people. We didn't *like* war, we just wanted to protect ourselves.

I looked at them. Before I couldn't see any similarities, but now, as I looked closer, they had a lot more in common than Deckard and I did. In Nagdecht, we often worried about them joining forces because of their lengthy history and similar genetics. Looking at the surface, I'd thought that they didn't look as related as we so often made them out to be, but the closer I looked, the more I noticed.

"What are you looking at?" Delmar asked as I stared at them.

"I was just thinking how similar you two look."

They both gave me queer looks, and I tried to explain, "You both have super-curly hair. We don't get curly hair in Nagdecht. And you both have straight ears ... his curl a little bit, but they're both straight up, and they don't move." I fingered the tip of my ear. Our type of ears didn't exist in Geuran and Rhodaren.

"And you both have really big noses. A lot bigger than ours, anyway."

My nose was much smaller. My hair was fine and straight. The more I thought about it, the more I saw it. Deckard and Delmar really were more alike. I felt more distant from Deckard than I had before. They had similar genes that weren't found in Nagdecht at all, even if superficially things looked different. Deckard even agreed with Delmar more often than he did with me.

They glanced at each other with expressions of disbelief. Deckard quirked a brow up. "I don't see it."

"Neither do I," Delmar agreed.

"There's just one thing. I don't get why Rhodarens are so fat."

Delmar flinched at my words. It took him a second to answer irritably, "I'm not fat."

"But you're so ..." I gestured towards his stomach. He was clearly bigger than I was.

"I'm telling you I'm not fat. You're just a twig."

"I'm not a twig. I'm a healthy weight!"

"You're barely in one piece. You could snap in half at any moment."

"I'm healthy! I'm a good 11.2, that's perfectly decent," I defended myself.

"A what?" He wrinkled his brow.

"11.2."

He looked at Deckard. Deckard shrugged in response.

"What's that supposed to mean?" he asked.

"The GICH test," I stated firmly. It occurred to me that they didn't take as much care as Naggians did with their genes. "11.2 is average. I'm perfectly healthy."

"Why are you talking about some test?"

"Because it shows how healthy people are!" I started to get exasperated. Sometimes it felt like the other countries didn't know a lot of normal things.

"I don't need a test to tell me I'm fine." Delmar glared at me, perplexed. He didn't get it at all.

I sighed, getting back to the subject. "But you clearly have extra weight on you."

He grumbled and stood up, and I panicked as he reached to grab the bottom of his shirt. "I'm not overweight." Before I had a chance to say anything he pulled it up.

I leaned back at first, shocked, but I could hardly help looking. Although he had a small amount of extra weight it wasn't nearly as much as I pictured. There was even a hint of an outline of his muscles.

He stiffly lowered back to the ground. I had to admit, I was wrong. Rhodarens just looked different.

"You're flushing." He raised his eyebrows at me.

"I'm not blushing!" I retorted.

"You're totally flushing." He smirked. He had an odd sense of confidence about his looks for a Rhodaren.

"I am not!" I looked to Deckard for confirmation. His gaze immediately snapped the other way and he ignored me. I grimaced. So much for my back-up.

"But, even you have to admit … You're still bigger than us. I don't get it. Why don't you guys worry more about your health?"

"I can tell you one thing," he answered. "You freeze in seconds."

"Wait, you mean …" It all came to me at once. "Of course, you guys have to keep warm, don't you?"

It suddenly made sense. They lived in snow constantly. They had to adapt for cold weather. I had been looking at it the wrong way the whole time. They didn't live in our climate. I felt like I finished a puzzle I didn't realize I was working on.

He stood and brushed himself off, giving the lympet sitting in the snow a command. "Keep an eye on these two."

She looked up at him and stayed in place. Her tail batted up once. He walked away from us, going through some trees. I looked at her. She looked at me. She didn't seem to care about our presence at all.

I crept from our camp over to the bushes to get a look at what Delmar was doing. He had his phone – audio only – up to his ear with his other arm wrapped around him.

Wondering if I would hear some vital information, I waited, but as I listened it became apparent he was talking to a lover on the other end. Faint giggles came from the phone.

"Don't worry about it. I might still be able to make some money."

I couldn't hear the other side of the conversation. All I could make out was indistinct chattering.

"Look, I know things haven't gone according to plan, but I'm trying to fix things. I might still be able to make up for it. Then we can get a little apartment in the city or something … I know, I know. Look, I'll help out. No … I know. It's going to be fine, don't worry."

As they talked, he started singing, slow and upbeat. His voice was a decent baritone. The style was much different than listening to auditions at the theater.

He lowered the phone and I scuttled away before he could spot me. I crawled back to the fire and sat next to Deckard, shoving some food into my mouth quickly.

He trudged through the snow and shoved the phone his pocket, stopping in front of the fire.

"So," he started, pausing. "Something you wanted to know?"

"Mph?" I asked, my cheeks full.

"Considering you felt like watching my phone call." He raised a brow and look down at me.

I swallowed a large chunk.

"Ah ... no ... was just curious ..." I explained weakly.

"She's my girlfriend," he stated bluntly.

"Oh, I see. But what was that money stuff about?" I asked.

"Is it that weird to want money?" He sat down beside me.

"No, but ... it sounded like you needed it for some reason."

"Heh, she's a farm girl. The original plan was to move to the city together, but her neighbors are having a little issue. And those farmers like to stick together. The western farmers practically speak their own language, too."

"What happened?"

"Seems the neighbor's parents died and they left everything to their oldest. But he's up and disappeared, and they can't find him anywhere. Only his name was on the inheritance and he vanished before he got to write a will or anything, so they're going to have issues if they can't find him. 'Course, if we get the money, we can always take care of that," he answered.

"That's weird. Why did he disappear?"

"Who knows? It's a farm. The property is worth a good amount, maybe someone did him in."

"Someone would kill him to take the farm?" I asked, stunned.

"People have killed for less, so why not?"

"I guess. Seems a little sad."

"I don't know the guy," he shrugged, "but she's not going to let anything happen to their family, so looks like our plans to move in together will have to wait awhile."

"I'm kind of surprised you have a girlfriend. I mean, you seem like kind of a flirt," I said.

He gave me a smug grin. "With looks like this it's an easy way to get information."

I stared at him. "With looks like that?"

"Of course. Sex appeal is an effective tool."

"Sex app ..." I didn't finish what I was saying. "Never mind. How did you meet a farm girl if they're such an insular community?"

"We bumped into each other in the city. Literally. I stopped on a street, and she bumped right into me. She thought my lympet was cute," his hand dropped on her head as he looked at her with a grin, "and we started talking. That funny way they talk was adorable."

"So you're just doing this for money? Why not some other sort of job?"

He sighed, but he didn't sound irritated. Rolling his shoulders, he folded his arms and sat back. "I was never much of one for a desk job or something. I like to move around. See the world. Odd jobs always made it easy enough to do that. That's why I got the truck."

So he liked to travel? Odd. I had something in common with a Rhodaren.

"I see. So you just like adventure or something?"

He laughed. "I guess you could say that." Lifting up his lympet, he lay on his back in the snow and held her up. Above his head, she hung like a limp noodle before she weakly placed her paw on his nose.

We stayed silent for a long time while he played with her, cooing over her like she was a baby. We still didn't even know how the man was connected to

182

Breigah. While it was on my mind, I decided to bring it up, "So ... we really don't know anything about this guy? Is there any other way we can look stuff up about him?"

Delmar's eyes dropped to his bag. "We got some of his stuff but it didn't help a lot."

Resting Feenie on his chest, he dug into his stuff with one hand and held it out for me.

"Is that his identification?" I asked. It was small and rectangular like a Naggian ID, but it didn't have any place on it for fingerprint identification. I couldn't tell if it could be used with electronic devices at all. I flipped it over, looking at both sides. It had his picture, a name, and a bunch of random information about him.

My ID had a small, clear piece on it so that when I inserted it into a machine it could take my thumbprint to confirm identification. It was how all of our IDs were made, except for people who were unable to identify themselves that way. It was strange seeing what looked like little more than a laminated piece of paper being the basis of how they proved their identity.

"How does someone confirm that this is them?" I asked.

"It has a picture on it," he answered.

"Yeah, but ... what about fingerprints? Or DNA? Can't someone really easily fake a picture?"

I turned it over in my hands and he took it from me, holding it closer to the fire as he examined it. He turned it on his side, looking at the edge.

"Most people don't do that kind of thing," he answered, eyes close to the card. "But this is fake."

"It is?" I asked, surprised. I had been arguing that it was easy to fake, but I hadn't suspected it was a fake. I'd never even seen a real one to compare it to. "How can you tell?"

"The lamination is shoddy," he explained. "If I messed with this enough it would probably come apart."

"Why don't you guys make a more complex ID system? It seems like these would be really easy to fake and commit crimes."

"And I suppose there's no crime in Nagdecht?" he jeered at me.

"Well ..." I paused. I knew well there was. I'd seen more than enough of it up close and personal. "I mean, of course there is, but we at least do our best to make it difficult to pull off. Our IDs use fingerprint identification when we use them, and our DNA is in the system if we ever need to be identified further."

He was about to reply when Deckard interrupted.

"Hey, guys," he said, holding up two hands between us. Somehow he always seemed to get stuck in the middle. "Shouldn't we be asking an obvious question here? Why would he be carrying a fake ID?"

"Because he wants to use a fake name," Delmar stated.

"You mean something like, he commits robberies and gets away with it by hiding under a new name?"

"It could be something like that, but it's also overlooking something."

"What?"

"The whole reason we didn't suspect that the husband did it before was because he had a different name than the person Breigah was going after. But if he's hiding under a fake name, it's perfectly possible this guy murdered his wife then took the kid and ran away."

"But why would he kill his wife?"

"She did mention she was going to sell his stuff behind his back, and it sounded like he was addicted to the stuff. Breigah even used it as a way to lure him out and find him. Maybe he found out what she was doing and they had an argument. Whatever the reason, I plan on finding him."

"What are you going to do when you find him?"

"I don't know," he answered.

Our conversation drifted off into silence, and I thought about what I'd learned. We slept in the back of the truck that night.

19
3, 13, 3399
Errday

She hobbled out of her door. The morning sun warmed her face. Some of the workers were already unloading feed. The smell of grain and horses permeated the air. She closed her eyes, bathing in the warm rays of the sun. Not a single flake of snow in sight. It was truly a beautiful day.

Her workers were gathered around the back of a large truck. One stood on the tailgate and slid lengthy trays out so that the other farmhands could reach them. Each tray was packed with fodder. When they pulled the fodder out, it curled up and folded like a strip of carpet covered in bright grass. She could tell it was good quality feed.

Nostalgia washed over her. She had spent many mornings unloading feed in her life. The workers began moving the fodder in a wheelbarrow to take it to the horses. Walking over, she moved another wheelbarrow. She hooked the handle of her cane on the back of the truck and dug her fingers into the soil. The sod was heavy, but slid across the tray smoothly and poured into the wheelbarrow. Soon it was full and ready to be taken to the horses.

She attempted to heft it up, but it was much heavier than she expected. As soon as she lifted it, she stumbled forward from the weight. The wheelbarrow nearly toppled over as she did her best to steady it again.

A farmhand hopped off the tailgate and held her arm, grabbing the side of the wheelbarrow with the other hand.

"Are you okay, Ma'am?" she asked.

She sighed, regaining her balance. "Yes, I'm fine. These are a bit heavier than I remember them."

"It's all right, Ma'am, we can get them."

The worker's hand lingered on her arm, holding her up. She let go of the handles and grabbed her cane again, "Yes, I suppose that's for the best."

She walked down the path, listening to the chirping of the birds. After six years, her husband's tree was about the same height as she was. It had thick foliage and was covered in small flowers.

Her eyes strayed to the small, flat stone a couple of feet away. It had an inscription on it that read, "Reserved for Breigah". She had carved the words into it and placed it there shortly after his death. She hadn't joined him quite yet, but she knew where she wanted to go.

One of her workers jogged down the road, wiping her forehead with a heavy glove. She had a set of letters in her hands.

She paused in front of Breigah and held them out, "Your mail came."

"Thank you," she accepted them. She shuffled towards her home as she flipped through them.

She settled down on her couch with the morning sun beaming through the window behind her. She set aside all of the letters but one. It came from Edalbeg, the city her daughter lived in. She furrowed her brows, seeing that it was from the same city, but wasn't from her daughter. Instead it seemed to be from the police.

Concerned, she ripped the envelope open and pulled out the letter.

We deeply regret to inform you of the passing of your daughter, Ardus. She passed in Hulsben in her home.

We would like to request that you come to Edalbeg. We have reason to believe that foul play was involved in her passing, and we believe you may have information that can help in the investigation.

It had the signature of the chief of police in Edalbeg.

A sense of disbelief overwhelmed her. It couldn't be. Her daughter wasn't involved in any illicit activity. Why would anyone hurt her? A robbery?

She didn't want to accept it. She tried to convince herself that it was a mistake, that if she went to Edalbeg it would turn out that it was someone else.

Her arms sank. She stared at the letter, stooping over as she couldn't pull her eyes away from it.

20
5, 15, 3399
Waddersday

When I woke up, it was to the truck shaking. I rubbed my eyes, looking for the source. Towards the front of the truck Delmar was scrubbing the floor hard. The lympet was still in the back of the truck, watching him. Her ears were slightly down. She looked a little guilty.

"What's going on?" I asked.

"Just cleaning up."

A slight smell made me wrinkle my nose, and I brought a hand up to shield it. "Did she pee in the back of the truck?"

"Hey, she has more right to pee in here than you have to sleep in here," he defended her.

I got up quickly. I didn't want to lie around a pile of urine.

"I don't understand why you keep that thing around anyway. It doesn't do anything," I grumbled at him.

"She does plenty," he snapped back.

"She doesn't even walk. You carry her." I flicked an ear.

"That's none of your business. You don't just throw out family when it's convenient."

I walked away in a snit, irritated and double checking to make sure that nothing had gotten on me. Fortunately, I was clean. As clean as a man who had barely bathed could be.

We set back out. After making a stop at the shed again, we took a break to go to the bathroom and stretch. Feenie was lying on her back on Delmar's lap while he played with her feet.

The snow scrunched beneath me as I walked out of their view. My mind felt numb as I went through the mechanical motions, barely taking in my surroundings. Without much thought, I noticed a snowmobile behind the shed several seconds before the significance of it hit me. My eyes darted around until I spotted movement.

I scanned the trees for an animal. Another movement caught my eye. It was a man hiding behind a tree. Confusion and fear swept over me, and they only grew when I realized he was the man from the house. When I spotted him, he knew he was caught.

A shovel was in his hand and I knew he had a gun. My heart leapt.

The second our eyes met, he took an aggressive step forward. I turned to run as fast as I could back to the truck. Deckard was standing behind it with Delmar. I grabbed Deckard's sleeve when I reached him. "That guy is out there! Come on, we need to hide!"

Deckard didn't ask for further explanation. He followed me as I zipped through more trees.

We only stopped half a minute later. It had completely slipped my mind that Delmar couldn't run. I spun on my heels to see what was happening.

The other man swung the shovel at Delmar. He blocked with his arm, but was knocked over. Deckard and I began running back but we had already put too much space between us and him.

"A rifle would be nice right now!" Deckard yelled at me.

"Not now, Deckard!"

"Just saying!"

Delmar was stuck on the ground as the other man approached. As much as he bore the pain before, he couldn't put much pressure on his leg. It showed when his leg trembled from the strain. There was no way he could pull himself up with someone chasing him.

The lympet darted by him. She growled before climbing up the other man's leg and biting him. He stumbled back, trying to get a grip on her as he panicked. He yanked her off by the scruff of her neck and flung her into a tree. She smacked it with a pitiful yelp, tumbling to the ground.

By then Delmar had gotten himself up and we were getting close. He charged the man and shoved him away. After a brief scuffle, the man fled. I paused next to Delmar to make sure he was okay. Deckard ran a couple yards farther but stopped before going behind the shed. Heart pounding painfully, I jumped back into action to join him and go after the man together.

It was all too fast that we heard the sound of the snowmobile. It flew right by us, shooting flecks of snow. I shielded my face with my arms and stayed back. There was no way we were going to catch him on that. After I watched to make sure he left, I headed back in a daze.

After the initial panic wore off, I saw Delmar next to the tree. He was cradling the lympet. I was surprised at first that I didn't hear a sound and assumed she must have already died. I watched a man who seemed to be so casual about death before bawl his eyes out as he petted her.

"It's okay ... you're going to be okay ..." He stroked her head again and again, his voice shaking. She wasn't dead. Her mouth moved to mewl, but nothing came out. She was a weak animal to begin with – being thrown against a tree was too much for her.

He continued petting her even as the small movements came to a stop, holding her close to his chest, unwilling to let her go.

It felt like an eternity passed before he gently set her down. Neither Deckard nor I wanted to interrupt him.

He grabbed the shovel and began digging a hole. She was small, so he didn't have to dig very deep. When he laid her in it, he took great care to put her in a comfortable spot, not letting any limb get twisted in any way.

My gaze darted around until it landed on a hard, lumpy round cone on the ground, dropped from one of the trees. I wasn't sure, but I imagined it had to be some sort of seed. Grabbing it, I ran it over to him to plant with her. Surprised when I appeared by his side, he raised an eyebrow at what I was holding, but he took it without a word. I retreated to give him space. As he buried her, he placed it on some of the dirt on top of her, then continued shoveling until the hole was filled.

It was reminiscent of how people were treated after death, although the body wasn't processed. He was treating her just like a Pressean.

The low singing filled the air again. This time I listened to the words.

"Cast away the shroud of cold ..." he went on. It was some sort of song about leaving the cold and finding the warmth beyond the mountains. His baritone voice was the only sound until he finished and we sat in silence while he knelt in front of her grave.

We waited a long time before he finally came over to us. "Let's get moving." The energy was drained from his voice.

I didn't want to ask about the song immediately. We sat in silence in the truck for a long time before I spoke up, "What was that song?"

"It's to help people find their way after they die, so they don't get stuck in their bodies. They're supposed to get out of the cold and follow the path up the mountains to the sun." His voice was sullen, sad, but composed. "Nadders don't sing?"

"No, we don't do that. Rhodarens don't plant seeds?" I asked. He hadn't gotten a seed from anywhere when he buried her.

"We do," he corrected. "But there are a lot of areas where there's no point in trying to plant something. You make do with what you can."

"But don't those kind of contradict each other? I mean, if the song is about the soul leaving, and the seed is about the soul staying in the plant ..."

"And all of your beliefs make perfect sense?"

I backed off. Many of our traditions were illogical. They stemmed from the beliefs people from ancient civilizations held, when they still believed in Pressea. Nowadays, most people didn't believe in the goddess, but the traditions lived on. I didn't have any strong beliefs myself, and seriously doubted that if someone's body was planted with a seed that their soul would be in the plant that grew. Yet, if something happened to Dad, I knew I would buy the absolute best seed I possibly could for him. Whether I believed it or not, it was just what we did, and I couldn't imagine how wrong it would feel if I didn't.

"I'm sorry ... It slipped my mind that you couldn't run." I still felt horrible about it. I'd run right by him and left him stuck there. If I hadn't, maybe this wouldn't have happened. Maybe we could have fended the man off.

"Yeah," he said, but it felt like he wasn't listening to me. He stared straight ahead. The rest of the drive went like that. It felt extremely long.

21
5, 12, 3399
Firsday

They drove through the forest. Delmar navigated through the trees carefully and slowly. They stopped nearby where they buried the box. She and Delmar climbed out of the truck. The other man pulled up on his snowmobile behind them.

Delmar opened the back of the truck then carried his lympet to some dry brush, setting her down. She sniffed at the snow before digging a small hole to create a makeshift bathroom.

Breigah walked to the back of the truck and met the other man. He pulled the shovel out of the back of the truck. "All right, now where do we dig?"

"It's this way." She led him to a spot with snow that had been previously disturbed. He held the shovel over his shoulder as they walked.

As he lowered the shovel to start digging, her hand slipped under her coat. Her fingers brushed the cold rim of her gun. He stabbed the ground with the shovel, setting a foot on top of the shoulder of the blade.

"Holf," she said softly.

"Hmm?" He turned his head, glancing back at her.

"You don't recognize me, do you?" she asked him.

"No. Should I?" he replied.

"I'm Ardus's mother," she told him. She ripped the gun from her waist and pointed it at him. He knew well not to stick around. He spun around and ducked behind the tree as fast as he could as two bullets came towards him.

Startled, Delmar jumped up with his lympet in hand.

The man pushed away from the tree and ran. Breigah kicked up snow as she gave chase.

Delmar glanced down at his lympet in confusion.

"Should we follow?" he asked, as if expecting an answer. The lympet looked up at him, mewling once pitifully. He packed her into her bag and sprinted after them.

The man was faster than her. She saw him slowly putting more distance between them the farther they ran. He made his way up a hill. The path was unstable and crumbling. Pebbles dislodged and rolled down the side as they ran across.

Her heart beat so fast, she felt like it could give out at any moment. Eyes forward, lungs dry from the chilly air, she did her best to keep him in sight, but she lost him among the trees when they reached the other side of the path. She continued, desperate to catch him. Trees passed by her in a blur.

A shovel swung at her. She barely saw it, raising her arms to protect herself as the man came out from behind a tree. She stumbled back and hit the ground. She raised the gun, but he grabbed her arm. They wrestled for the firearm. She was dragged to her feet, fumbling in the snow as he yanked and shoved her. Her other hand came around to grab the weapon, clinging onto it desperately.

He bashed into her with the full force of his weight. She fell backwards and he fell on top. Her arm shook. As hard as she held on, her muscles struggled to stay clenched. Her fingers ached. He punched her, and she attempted to block with her arms.

The metal scraped her fingers when she lost her grip. As soon as her hand gave away slightly, the gun was ripped away from her.

The man pulled back from her quickly, throwing his arm up with the gun to hold it away from her. She sat up on her elbow, unable to jump back to her feet as quickly.

She looked up at the man. He pointed the gun down at her. For a brief moment they looked at each other. Her glare was full of hatred.

Two shots rang out.

22

5, 15, 3399
Waddersday

Smoke billowed from the trees in the distance as we pulled up to the greenhouse. When we got closer, we saw the woman again, but this time she was outside, running towards the lake and carrying some heavy equipment. It was a hose. She hastily tried to set it up and run it out towards the fire that was eating through the dead trees.

I jumped out as soon as the truck pulled to a stop, shouting at the woman, "We need to get out of here!"

Deckard climbed out behind me, and Delmar limped around from the other side. One hose would have difficulty fighting the fire.

"I can't!"

"You can find another place, you need to get somewhere safe!" I sprinted through the snow over to her.

"I can't!" she shouted back, still setting up her hose to fight the fire.

We stopped, shocked, and darted over to help. She shoved the hose into my arms and started up the engine.

The hose was massive, and when she started it up, the strength of it nearly knocked me over. I held onto it by pressing it against my chest and clinging to it as hard as I could. Deckard grabbed it to help. Delmar finally limped up. His weight helped control it.

As we frantically sprayed water around to protect the area she glanced behind us and something caught her attention. She suddenly darted towards the greenhouse, yelling, "Stop!"

I spun around. While we were all focused on the fire, the man had approached the greenhouse behind us. She ran towards him to fend him off but he pulled out a gun. Immediately she stepped back, holding her hands up, seeming desperate to both stop him and not get killed all at once.

Fearing for her safety, I dropped the hose and ran towards them. When I was half way, Deckard dropped it to come after me.

"Are you serious?" Delmar yelled out as he was left alone to man the massive hose.

The closer I got, the more I realized I didn't have a plan of action. What was I going to do against a gun? I stopped a distance from him, hesitant to get any closer. But when he went to the door the woman panicked. She lunged at him, grabbing his arm before he had a chance to aim the gun again. He slammed her against the wall and she hit her head, falling to her knees. I was forced back into action. I rammed him but it felt like bouncing off a wall.

He grabbed me and hurled me. I lost my balance and rolled in the snow. Catching myself, I jumped back to my feet.

A shot suddenly rang out. I stepped back once. I looked down at my body and saw blood. Somehow, I didn't feel the pain in that moment; maybe I was in too much shock. I remembered how Breigah had died after being shot in the gut. I couldn't tell exactly where the blood was coming from. I pressed a hand to my midsection and lifted it, covered in blood.

Suddenly I collapsed to the ground, fighting to keep from going unconscious. Deckard wrestled with him above me. Grabbing the arm with the gun, he tried to pull it from him. Everything felt wobbly.

Deckard wasn't that much bigger than I was. I watched him struggle in the fight. The man hit him into the wall. I was shaking. He was going to kill all of us. I floundered on the ground with my wound. I didn't want him to kill Deckard, but I couldn't find the strength to get back up.

Suddenly, I was awash in a shower of water. I covered my face from the initial shock. A strong jet of water knocked the man down. Delmar had turned the hose on him and the force was more than enough to shove him over.

Deckard had a chance, and jumped on top of him, wrestling with the gun. Another shot rang out. I winced and lowered my ears. Something thumped on the ground next to me. When I opened my eyes, it was the man. Deckard was holding the gun. Panting, I watched the man as he stopped moving, then stopped breathing.

For a while, time seemed to be frozen. I lay there next to a body, numb both mentally and physically. Delmar turned the hose back towards the incoming fire.

My vision faded and I felt faint. All I knew for sure was that I was shot and bleeding. Deckard dropped down to a knee next to me. I was holding myself up on one elbow and starting to slump backwards. He scooped me up, and a flash of pain shot through me.

I clung onto consciousness but everything got farther and farther away. Voices sounded so distant and everything got dark. Everything felt surreal. Things went from cold to warm. I had an odd sting of pain. Time seemed to swirl around me. I couldn't tell how much was passing. Then I died. Or at least it felt like it.

When I became aware I was lying on a table inside. Even though a chill ran over me, it seemed like the room was heated. I felt weak as I looked around. Deckard was standing by the table.

"How long has it been ...?" I squeezed my eyes shut as I tried to sit up.

"Probably a bit over an hour. I did what I could, I think I got it okay, but you need to go to a real hospital. All we had was a first aid kit."

Wrapping an arm around me, he helped me sit up. I held my stomach as it ached. Delmar was standing to the side of the room. The woman was standing in the doorway.

"The fire?" I asked.

"We got it out with water and some good old Rhodaren snowfall," she said.

"And what about ... the guy?" I asked.

"He sprayed him into the lake." She pointed her thumb at Delmar. "Seemed to have something major against him."

"He killed my lympet," he answered bluntly, as if no further explanation was needed.

"Oh, I see," she answered. Somehow that seemed to make sense to both of them.

"That just leaves the statue then," I said.

"You're going to have to give up finding that statue," Deckard told me.

I sat up taller. "I don't think so."

"But I don't know if you're going to be okay. We don't have time to run around looking for it."

"I'm pretty sure it's here."

He blinked at me in shock.

I turned my eyes from him to the woman. "The actual statue is probably still here."

Moving my legs to hang them off the side of the table was a greater challenge than I thought possible. Every movement bothered my stomach. Deckard fidgeted around me. When I tried to stand on my own, I quickly discovered it would be impossible. He grabbed onto me, supporting most of my weight. Clenching my teeth, I waited for the pain to subside a bit before turning my eyes to the woman.

She looked ready to run, shrinking back.

"It's true," she answered quietly.

"Wait, what?" Delmar took more interest. "What's going on here with that box and stuff?"

She grimaced, looking at a desk before going over to it and browsing through some paperwork. "All she wanted were the documents for it. She showed me this."

Delmar moved to take a look at it and Deckard instantly walked away, but I couldn't stand on my own. I leaned on the table.

"What is it?" I asked impatiently. They both glanced at it before Deckard carried it over to me. It was an article about the murder.

"She told me that her daughter was murdered and her granddaughter was kidnapped, and the guy who did it was obsessed with collecting rare things. All she wanted was the paperwork so that she could pretend she had it and lure him out." Her eyes met mine for a brief second. "I didn't plan on selling it, so I didn't need it, anyway. That man must have realized that and set the fire to make me come out."

I stared at the article. So many were dead.

Delmar broke through my thoughts as he demanded more answers, "What did you get it appraised for, if you weren't planning on selling?"

She took a step back from him. Though she didn't look weak based on the musculature of her arms, she did seem timid. "I did plan on it, but then I couldn't." Her gaze darted to the door momentarily.

"Well, I'm sick of this." Delmar limped towards the door. "I'm finding out what's in here."

"No!" the woman shouted, getting in his way. "At least give me a chance to explain."

"Explain what?"

Her eyes darted behind her where Delmar was trying to go, before she gave up with a sigh. "I'm a botanist. I've been going into Lyruna to find and preserve rare plant species so I can study them." I leaned heavily against the table, wondering what the big deal was.

"When I was out last time, I found the remains of a tendril monster village. The entire place had been destroyed." For a moment her eyes met mine. "By soldiers. They had destroyed villages that were too close to civilization."

It sounded like what our soldiers did. Tendril monsters were extremely dangerous, and we had to make sure they didn't start invading our territory.

"I looked around what was left and found a garden. Most of it was gone but a few sprouts had begun blooming. They must have still been under the earth when the village was destroyed." She nervously looked around at all of us as she continued. "So, I dug them up and brought them here. I had to find out what the tendril monsters were gardening."

She paused, and I was struck by my curiosity, "Well … what was it?"

With furrowed eyebrows, she hesitated to respond. "I didn't know what they were until a couple of weeks later. They grew into large bulbs, and then the petals fell away … They were little tendril monsters." She became more defensive. "That's why I couldn't let anyone in. If people found out they were here, they'd be killed."

"Wait," Delmar was stunned, "you're telling me there's tendril monsters in there?"

"They're not dangerous. They can't even walk yet," she explained. "That's why I couldn't leave. They can't move yet, and I can't pull them out without risking their lives. They're too small and weak."

We exchanged looks before Deckard helped me walk into the other room. The greenhouse was just as large as it looked from the outside, and the main portion of it was one giant room with a glass ceiling. Plants of all kinds were potted or planted in dirt areas on the ground.

In the middle, there was a large basin full of dirt, with nine tiny tendril monsters. Four were planted in a square, and the other was a group of five. They looked like Presseans buried from the waist up, except their skin was green and their "hair" was made of vines, with the occasional flower growing on them. It reminded me of Valli and the flowers he wore in his hair. Most looked sprightly, but one appeared to be wilting. Their bodies were thin and tiny. They were probably only three inches high from the waist. Large petals lay flat on the dirt around them, like natural skirts. Below that had to be their roots.

They were much too small to be threatening. A few swayed. They let out small squeaks, not forming any sort of words. Some began turning their eyes our way, and the alert ones squeaked noisily in response. Deckard helped me to get closer to see.

I reached out a finger to one. Its tiny hands wrapped around my finger. With seemingly no goal, it touched my finger curiously, before it opened its mouth and attempted to bite the tip. Luckily, it seemed to have no teeth. If they had been full grown, I would have been terrified being this close to them, but they were so fragile that I couldn't help but feel for them. They were completely helpless.

"Aww, it's trying to eat me." I chuckled, restrained. Moving my chest too much hurt. I perked an ear and glanced at her, a question suddenly troubling me. "... Do they eat people?"

I hadn't heard of them eating people before, but there were plenty of stories about them attacking people.

Her expression fell and she grimaced. "Ah ... no. They can't digest meat, it seems. I ..." She looked surprisingly upset about it. Her gazed flicked over to the tendril monsters. "I gave Duren a small piece of meat and he became very ill. I had to go purchase a first aid kit so that I could get the meat out of his stomach. It was pretty difficult but ... I'm hoping he gets better."

Looking at them again, I took note of the one that looked like he was wilting. So Duren was the sick one? That explained why. A sharp pain stung my heart seeing such a small creature in pain. The other one was still trying to gnaw on my finger.

"Then why is it biting me?"

"I guess because he's a couple of months old. He tries to eat everything."

I let out a small, amused huff. "They're cute."

"They get a lot bigger," Deckard said, reserved. Even as he helped me stand, he tried to stay away from them. "Aren't you worried they'll attack you when they get bigger?"

"They're very intelligent, just like us. As long as I don't do anything to them, I shouldn't have any reason to worry."

"But they're known for attacking people."

She put a hand to her chin. "I haven't figured out quite why that is yet. I have some theories, but they're too young to tell. I believe the reason they imitate us is some form of commensalism – that is, they need us for some reason. But it can't be for everyday living because we would be attacked much more often."

I scrutinized them. They had differences. Different colored flowers on their heads, different body

209

types, and different faces. One had a trimmer waist and very small bumps on its chest. When I realized what they were, I was surprised to see them on a creature so young.

"That one is a girl?"

She shook her head. "So far it looks like they're all the same gender. That is, they're all both. Those differences are shallow. Just imitating us. I've done scans, and they don't seem to serve any purpose beyond that."

I tilted my head. So they were all both genders? Weird.

The more she explained, the more excited she got, and she offered more, gaining more confidence. "It's all fascinating, really. You see the way they're planted, in sets of four?"

"But there's five there."

"I did that, because one was extra. They were originally planted in sets of four. At first, I didn't understand why. It seems like it would cause more competition for root growth and I didn't see any benefit. But when they finally bloomed, it made sense." She held her hands around them. "Look. They're being socialized."

"They are?"

"Yes! Their infants are stuck to the ground for a long amount of time. They can't walk or crawl, and they can't be picked up without a chance of harming their roots. They're planted together like this so they can play with each other!"

It held onto my finger, but I easily out-maneuvered it and pulled away gently. Instead, it grabbed onto the edge of its own petal, pulling it up from the dirt and biting on the end.

This explained a lot. She didn't want to call for help because she was hiding these little guys. Much like us, Rhodarens culled tendril monsters near the edges of Lyruna. It was to protect our people from their attacks, but seeing the little ones made me feel badly. They looked so innocent and helpless. Did the soldiers really cull them with the rest?

I hoped for her sake that she was right and they wouldn't grow up to be violent.

I glanced up at her. "And the statue?"

She glanced down a moment before walking over to an area covered in pots. Picking one up, she set it down on a table. It was old and had an odd shape, having a bulbous bottom with two pointy, unusually placed handles, then coming up to form a large opening. I glanced at it and looked up at her. It was a dirty old thing, emptied of dirt but stains showed it had been filled for a long time.

After a second, she flipped it over. It wasn't a pot. Suddenly the handles became ears. The bulbous bottom was a head. The large opening was the chest area. Massive erosion had defiled the whole thing. But I could still see the face.

"It was in the ruins of their village. When I first came back, I was excited and had it checked out. But after they blossomed ... I realized this was one of the few things they have from their home, and I wanted to keep it for them." She pushed it forward on the table towards us. "But you helped save them, and I'm sure they'll understand if I give it to you."

Clinging to Deckard for support, I stumbled forward to look at the statue. Unlike the necklace, I felt positive that this was the real thing. Hundreds of years of experience were written all over it. The flute had been interesting. The necklace had just been something else to go after besides trinkets. This ... this was real history.

I touched the cheek on the statue. It was cold. We might not even know who this long deceased general was anymore. Without more to the statue, I couldn't tell if it was a man or a woman. Any paint had long worn off.

"Why would this be in a tendril monster village?" I asked.

"I'm not sure. From my understanding, it's some sort of statue from Nagdecht. But I don't know how they would have gotten their hands on it."

"It's a statue of a general from a long time ago," I explained. "From before the line of royals changed."

Everyone stared at me and I realized no one else here would know Naggian history. "The previous line of kings and queens. A long time ago they became corrupt, and wasted money and the people were living in terrible conditions. General Luenlore assassinated the king and replaced him, and that's where the current line of royals comes from." I gestured towards the statue. "This is a statue of one of the generals who came before General Luenlore. They were all destroyed and thrown out at some point."

"Ooh …" she answered as if she had a sudden revelation. I turned my eyes to her with a curious hum. "So they were erasing the previous generations and replacing them. Throwing out the old. That makes more sense, then. The Nadders destroyed the statues and disposed of them. Perhaps they even threw the pieces in or near Lyruna. The tendril monsters picked it up at some point and used the hollow part to garden with. If we assume the different villages communicate, this statue was traded over time and ended up all the way over here."

It was fascinating. Maybe the most interested I'd been in history besides stories about Tevias.

"You're sure we can have it?" My mind struggled with it. For the tendril monsters, this was a piece of what remained of their home. But it was part of our history, too. An important part, and we could probably learn something from it.

"Yes. I'm sure I can find more things for them if I keep looking."

I looked at Deckard, then Delmar. Delmar had been standing back with his arms folded.

"Can you carry that okay?" I asked them. I was too injured to do it. Delmar wasn't in great shape either, but he kept stubbornly chugging along. I had to admit some admiration for his gumption, especially when I was in pain now, too, and I only wanted to lie down.

"Yeah, sure," Deckard answered, escorting me to a seat and helping me sit down gently. He walked over to the statue with Delmar a step behind, and they hefted it up to take it to the truck. I didn't want to attempt to walk by myself yet and it gave me a chance to ask a question.

"Hey," I called her attention to me. "Can I ask you something?"

"Sure." She tore her eyes away from the saplings. If that's what they could be called.

"Earlier, when Delmar said that he was mad because his lympet was killed, it sounded like that was enough explanation for you. What's that about?" I asked.

"What do you mean?" She gave me an odd look.

"I mean, you don't find it odd that he's so attached to a lympet?"

"Of course not. People always are."

I fought to understand her, but I still felt like I was missing a clear answer. "Why?"

"It's just natural. I mean, he would have had it since he was a baby."

"Really? How can you be sure?"

"You don't know?" We both looked at each other in confusion. It was as if she knew some greater truth that I'd somehow overlooked my entire life, and she could hardly believe I hadn't noticed it.

"No, lympets are just considered pests at home."

"Pests?" she repeated, shocked. "Why would you think that? They're one of the most loyal creatures you can find."

"That's just the way it is." I shrugged. I had no explanation. "But what is it like over here?"

"Well ..." she paused, glancing up. "Generally, lympets are bought for infants. When the lympet is just a few weeks old it'll be put in the same room as the baby. It's a lot of work taking care of both for a while so not everyone does it, but they're known for forming a strong bond, and once they're big enough, they'll let parents know if something is wrong. Like if a baby stops breathing. Sort of like a natural alarm system. And they stay pretty close, so they're a great pet for people to have. They'll die to save their owners. He seems a bit old to have a lympet, though. His must have been ancient."

Rhodarens had a whole different view of lympets. I never even thought of them as pets before. They were just animals that dug up gardens and messed up compost heaps, leaving a trail of rubbish behind them.

"That's ... a lot different than at home."

"Chances are he's never been more than a few feet from it his entire life. They go with people to stores and schools and pretty much everywhere. It's only natural he would be attached."

I ran it through my head. The lympet would have been present every moment of his life. Losing her must have left a void. His bond, the way he treated her, made a lot more sense now.

The other two came back into the room. We had the statue. It was finally time for Deckard and me to

214

head back to our countries. I wanted to linger behind in the greenhouse for a bit, but we had no time to waste because of my injury. Deckard stayed with me, keeping an eye on me.

The ride was long, and the silence so thick that I felt like I had to break it or I'd be smothered. Every time I looked up, Delmar was staring straight ahead.

"Are you okay?" I asked.

His eyes looked dark, like the spark in them had gone out.

"I knew she was going to go soon."

I didn't know what to say, so I listened.

"A couple of years ago, I was walking to the store, and when I looked back she was way behind. She couldn't keep up with me anymore, so I took her to the vet, but she was just getting old. I started carrying her more, and then her body started shutting down, she started to have bladder problems, and after a while she was losing interest in food ..."

He described a long, painful process of watching her go downhill. I lowered my ears.

"I just wanted her to stick around a little while longer. We still had so much to do."

My injury gave me an excuse to delay my response as I struggled to breathe. I took in a few painful breaths, trembling as my entire torso stung.

"I'm sorry," I finally said. What else was there to say? I closed my eyes and we returned to silence.

23

5, 17, 3399
Firsday

The drive felt surprisingly quick as I drifted in and out of consciousness. Once in a while, we ate a little food, but I never stayed up long. Delmar drove us back to the border where we left Deckard's truck.

When we got out, Deckard hefted the statue onto the back of his vehicle before helping me out. I leaned heavily on him, holding onto my stomach. The door to the truck was open and I sat on the edge. Delmar and Deckard stood next to it as we said our good-byes.

"I'm going to have to make up the money somewhere else." Delmar sighed, exasperated at his lengthy work and non-existent pay.

"Hey, Delmar ..."

"Hnn?"

"I think you should watch over the little girl."

He looked at me oddly. "Maybe you didn't notice this, but I'm not exactly daddy material."

"But both of her parents and her grandmother are dead. She's going to need someone to check in on her." I lifted a finger towards him. "Besides, I thought you were all about Rhodaren honor, or something like that."

He waved his hands dismissively at me, annoyed even as he agreed, "All right, all right. I can make sure she's somewhere safe or something."

"Good."

We stared awkwardly for a moment, no one knowing what to say before Deckard spoke up, "This is something, isn't it?"

"What is?" I asked.

"A Geuranian, a Nad – Naggian, and a Rhodaren all together at the border. Bet that's never happened before."

It was weird. How had I let that slip my mind? I guess so much was going on that I wasn't thinking about it. Delmar placed a hand on his hip and gave an amused huff. "You're probably right about that. I hope I don't see any more Nadders crossing over the border."

"Hey!" I pouted at him.

"No offense, but if more come knocking on our door, it probably means Geuran is gone and we're the only ones left." He shook his head, throwing a hand up in a sloppy shrug. "I'm not big on Geuranians, but that doesn't mean we want to be next in line to go up against you guys."

I furrowed my eyebrows. Was that how Rhodarens thought? That if we defeated Geuran we would immediately go after them?

"We don't have any reason to attack you guys. You've never really done much to us," I protested, trying to reassure him.

"Yeah," his tone was dismissive as he waved me off. "I'm sure you guys would find a reason if you felt like it."

For a second, I wondered if that was true. But no. We had good reason to fight with Geuran. Naggians weren't warmongers. We wouldn't support attacking a country without good cause.

"It's not like you have to worry about that. We're still here," Deckard butted in, arms folded, one eyebrow raised as we casually dismissed his country.

"We all know if it goes to all-out war, you guys are going to lose," Delmar told him. Deckard's expression was grim, but he didn't protest. It was true. We massively outnumbered them and were better armed. Thinking on it now, I wasn't sure why we hadn't already crushed them after they attacked us a few years ago. We constantly had skirmishes at the border but we didn't advance on them. It was like we were playing it safe, waiting for something. Not that I was complaining. If we attacked, Deckard would be dead.

"Are the Rhodarens planning on doing something?" I asked.

"We haven't really decided yet … No one wants to get involved, but, no one wants you guys to be our neighbors, either." He gave me a pointed look.

My gaze dropped to the ground. "I wish we could just have peace," I mumbled.

Delmar sighed and shook his head, saying what we all knew. "That's never going to happen."

No matter how much any of us wanted it, the dark reality was hanging over our heads. They attacked us and killed people, then we attacked them and killed more people, and then they attacked us and killed people … It was never ending and people were always out for revenge. I recalled my dad and how badly he wanted to help protect the border after the capital had been attacked. He "wanted to protect Naggians from the Geuranians." There was no easy way about it. He had every reason to be there to fight, even if he would just be part of another generation repeating history. How were we ever going to break such a merciless cycle of hatred?

"Well then, see you, Nadder." Delmar threw a hand in the air dismissively as he turned.

"Naggian!" I snapped at him.

"Whatever. Naggian."

I cracked a smile, letting out a small, amused huff even though it hurt. "Just in time for us to never see each other again."

He glanced back at me with a smirk, but his hand dropped by his left side, checking for a bag that was usually there before falling straight.

That said, it was finally time to go. As I pushed myself up into the seat and Deckard moved towards the door to close it, Delmar began shuffling away. Our gazes repeatedly met as I would adjust myself inside the truck and look out again. This was it. I might not ever see a Rhodaren again.

"You should lie down. I'll take it easy driving," he told me.

"There's not much space to lie down here."

"It's fine. Just use me as a pillow."

I stretched out more than I had before, resting my head on him. My torso ached. He started the engine up, and, as he promised, he accelerated slowly. Soon we were back on the path towards Cerna, where I could get a ride back into Nagdecht. There was no way I could walk back, so it was my best option.

It was a horrendously long trip, but at least it wasn't cold. I used my coat as a blanket instead of wearing it. The truck constantly went over small bumps and I felt every one. Deckard's hand fell on my arm and he drove with one hand.

I closed my eyes. I had trouble sleeping, so I daydreamed about my graduation. Dad had come home. Since I lived in the capital, the ceremony was held in the castle. I sat among thousands of others in the hall while someone high up in the education system gave a speech. I didn't even know who she was. The students were placed in the middle of the room. On either side of us, there were seats for friends and family.

As was traditional, I wore all white. I tried to keep my gaze fixed on the front, but it wandered often to the side, where my dad was. My eyes strayed again and again. He continuously focused on the speaker until one time I looked towards him and caught his eye. I paused, cracking a smile. He smiled softly back and looked ahead again.

My chest swelled with pride. I could hardly bring myself to pay attention to the speech. After the first speaker, the king appeared on the stage to give a brief, optimistic speech about our futures and how the nation was counting on us to be productive citizens. My leg bounced up and down. His speech was mercifully short, and then it was time to get our mantles. We waited for the students who didn't have anyone there to make it to the front and be presented with their mantles. Then we were invited to stand and go get ours.

My heart was pounding when I squirmed through the crowd over to my dad. I navigated through the sea of people and found myself in front of him, looking up. He smiled and held up the mantle he had gotten for me. It was brown with some embroidery on the edge that mimicked vines. He slipped it over my head.

When I glanced at the crowd I saw many pink mantles and an assortment of other colors. I knew the brown likely came from my love of geography. It had always been something I did well in. Pinks were future police and soldiers. Each color had positives associated with it, picked out and ordered by parents for the graduation. It could represent something they had excelled at in school, loved, or planned on doing in the future.

I ran my thumb across the embroidery of my mantle. Dad had gotten it because of school, but it reminded me of the places I had traveled. I had been exploring our country and getting to know it on a hands-on basis. Not to mention Geuran. And now Rhodaren. Our map meant a lot more than some scribbles on a piece of paper now.

It was perfect for me. I wanted to be that traveler, a man who knew the land. Just thinking of it made my heart soar.

Dad only had the day to spend with me so we opted to celebrate at the castle. His arm was wrapped around me, gripping my shoulder as we walked. When we took the elevator to the dining halls we found it was crowded with other families.

We went out onto the walkways around the castle. It was probably sixty or seventy feet from the ground. There was a little table near the corner and we sat down to talk.

The conversation I could hardly remember. I only recalled the feeling of joy being there with him, and seeing him look so proud. A colorful little pufferbird landed on our table. It waddled towards me and puffed out its chest, making it look like an oversized ball of fluff.

I chuckled. "He's trying to intimidate me."

"I hear that scientists think it actually does that to be cute," Dad had answered. "That they adapted to live around us and it's a way for them to get food."

True or not, they were adorable birds. It was bright reds, yellows and blues, and seemingly fearless when I reached out to brush a finger over the fuzz on its chest.

That was when we noticed people clamoring outside and jogging towards the inner parts of the castle. Dad and I watched for a while before following to see what was going on. All around the walkway, people were gathered by the fence and watching the courtyard. We I leaned on the fence and looked down.

General Glaive and Dorrius were fencing in the courtyard.

"They're quite good," Dad commented. People around us were chattering excitedly. I glanced around and looked back down.

I had seen General Glaive fight seriously before. I got the feeling that they were playing, much to the joy of the new graduates. It was almost like watching an aggressive dance.

They *were* quite good. Almost too good. General Glaive and Dorrius had a history and this probably wasn't their first time sparring. They could react before they even saw anything coming.

King Lakorian was on the ground with them, standing on a walkway that surrounded the courtyard. He leaned on one of the fences. The Melechtions were on the other side. When I strained my ears I could hear them rooting for Dorrius.

We stayed there and got sucked up into the excitement. For a short time, it seemed like Dorrius might actually beat General Glaive. *An act*, I thought. Sure enough, General Glaive turned things around and had Dorrius pinned.

I remembered the feel of Dad's hand clapping my shoulder and the warmth of his body. It brought a smile to my face while I rested my cheek on Deckard's leg. I just had to make it to Nagdecht. Once I got home everything would be fine. I could go to the hospital and rest as long as I needed. Maybe Rykiel and Valli could visit me at home. Eyes closed, I pictured my nice cozy bed. Talking to Dad. Playing some cards with Valli. Having lunch with Rykiel. If the bullet hadn't killed me yet, I could probably hold on, and then everything would be fine.

The statue … It was so old. It didn't feel right to pawn it off. I'd talk to Ellora when I got back and see if we could make a deal with a museum or something. That was more like what I had always planned on doing.

When Deckard stopped to get food, I would lie down on grassy fields and wait for him to come back. He brought more food and drinks than he did on the way to Rhodaren, and I was grateful that they included healthier things. He picked up a little cart for me to carry the statue on, too. I made a mental note to do something to pay him back one day.

Then we'd be back to driving. He didn't go back to his military camp. Instead, he headed straight for Cerna. After days of driving, the high walls of Cerna were a welcome sight, and I ran it through my head over and over that I would be in a hospital soon.

He stopped a distance away to make sure the guard outside wouldn't recognize him. He helped me stumble around the truck on the opposite side, where the guard wouldn't see us at all. My wound had closed up in the time we'd been driving but it felt terrible, like I was constantly being punched in the gut while walking. Deckard placed the statue on the cart and then it was up to me.

"I'll go to Tenfort after this, north west from here. I'm sure you could find it if you need to."

I smiled. "Yeah. I guess I'll see you."

It was good-bye again. A painful good-bye. My fingers gripped the handle of the cart tightly as I leaned on it instead of Deckard and dragged myself to the entrance. We had already attracted the attention of the guard. He was a Geuranian, and he gave the truck and me a suspicious glare. Deckard was back in the driver's seat, watching.

Walking was painful. The bullet might have gone somewhere in my side, but every part of my body seemed to ache along with it. I made it to the guard and stood up as straight as I could without aggravating my injury.

"I need to get into the city," I said.

"Not from the Geuranian side you aren't. What do you think you're doing over here?" he demanded.

"Does it matter? I just want in," agitation leaked through my voice. I was in too much pain to hold it back.

"Letting Nadders in from the Geuranian side is against the rules," he informed me.

I stared at him. "What? Since when?"

"Since we had an issue a couple of years ago. No Nadders on this side, no Geuranians on the other side."

I flinched. Looks like they noticed that I entered the city twice a couple of years back and made a new rule.

"Why are you on this side?" he became more demanding. "I'll inform the army."

"Okay, okay, calm down. I'll go on the other side ..." I backed off. I needed to get away before he did something. I stumbled back to the truck. Deckard looked confused.

"What happened?" he asked, worried.

"They won't let me in on this side. I'll have to walk around to the other side."

"You can't walk all that way!"

"I don't have much choice." I breathed heavily. This was going to be painful.

"Get in the truck. I'll drive you there." He was already shifting to start the truck.

"Ah ..." I stared at him, mouth agape for a second. "But what if someone spots you? You could get caught driving around a Geuranian army vehicle on Naggian territory."

"It's fine. It's not that far across the border. I can drive away if I have to. Come on, get in." It was no longer a suggestion but an order. As much as I didn't want to put him out, I was in no shape to go on foot. Walking around the entire city would probably take hours if I was in good shape. In this shape, I would probably fall over and twitch on the ground until someone found me. I climbed back into the truck and he helped me pull the statue in.

Both of my arms were wrapped around my stomach as he drove me around the city. When we crossed the border, I tensed up. We weren't likely to run into anyone until we got to the entrance but I kept watch the whole way. He had an arm around me as he drove.

When we pulled up to the Naggian entrance there were a few other Naggians in line. Again we stopped a distance away – but the Geuranian army vehicle attracted attention anyway. I hoped for Deckard's sake that he could get away before anyone contacted the authorities.

I reluctantly pulled away from him, getting out with the statue to make another attempt at getting into the city.

Stumbling along, I stopped and glanced back. He was keeping an eye on me from the truck. I pursed my lips.

I wasn't going to make the same mistake twice. I limped back to the truck. As I approached he leaned forward, concerned.

"What's wrong?" he asked when I stood at the passenger side.

"I need some paper and a pen," I said.

We found a wrinkled scrap in our supplies. Scribbling quickly on it, I handed my address over to him.

"Maybe if you stop by Cerna sometime you can send me a letter or something," I suggested. I knew he couldn't give an address back to me. He moved around too much.

He took it, and smiled softly. "Yeah." I felt relieved. There was still a possibility of contact. Our ties weren't cut like they were two years ago.

I made my way to the entrance. Some of the other Naggians were on their v-phones and I hoped they weren't calling someone to go after Deckard. My eyes darted back at the truck. He was waiting for me to get in; I needed to hurry so he would go. I ignored the looks they gave me and stayed focused on getting inside the city.

It was a Naggian guard at the entrance this time. She glared at me, obviously suspicious of me like the others were, but she didn't have any reason to deny me entrance. As I stepped towards the city, I glanced back to see Deckard pulling away.

I had one major goal inside the city. Get to the post office. All I needed to do was mail the statue to Ellora and I could hitch a ride to the nearest Naggian city to get treatment. I couldn't drag the statue around with me. It was too big. Mail would probably be fine, though.

Waiting in the lines and filling out paperwork was grueling. I set it to be paid for by the receiver since I didn't have any money and waited an agonizingly long time for it to be my turn. I didn't wait for a Naggian. A Geuranian window opened up and I went straight to her.

She seemed surprised, but I got it processed and was free of the statue. I went straight from the post office to arrange a ride to the nearest city. When I finally boarded a vehicle, relief washed over me. Just a bit longer.

When I arrived at the hospital I threw myself into their care, ready to lazily accept anything they said. The wound had to be re-opened to remove some remnants, but it was stitched closed again, and I had to move with care to make sure I didn't irritate it. It was strange looking at my stomach with the clear stitches holding my skin together. They were rubbery and stretchy, like dried glue, but my body was supposed to absorb them after a while. Much of the time passed by with me drowsy from painkillers.

In a daze I remembered asking, "What day is it?" before I got ready to go home.

"Windsday," the nurse had told me.

Windsday ... Windsday ... It must have been the twenty-first. I was gone over four weeks. Maybe Dad was already back and trying to get a hold of me. I stumbled out of the hospital, renting a hovercraft despite the high price. I didn't care. I was ready to be back home. It didn't take long to get to the border of the capital that way, and before long, I was sitting in a cart riding to my final stop.

Walking from the cart drop-off to my house took longer than normal. The door to my house was a welcome sight. Hobbling towards it as fast as I could, I was just grabbing the door knob when someone called for me.

I did my best to feign that I was fine, looking to see who it was. Rykiel waved at me down the street and began jogging towards me. Perfect timing. I hoped he hadn't been checking the house too often.

"Leander!" he trotted up to me with a concerned expression.

When did he notice I was gone? I was going to have to figure it out.

"Oh, hi, Rykiel." I smiled, biting back the pain I was in.

"Where have you been? I've been trying to find you for days!" he asked, more urgent than normal. I hadn't expected him to notice I was missing so quickly.

I held back the panic. I could make up some sort of excuse for a few days, but how many had it been? "I've just been at a friend's house, that's all." I flashed him a nervous smile and got back to opening the door.

"Leander." He paused abruptly. I glanced at him. My excuse didn't seem to alleviate any of his concern at all. I thought I was hiding my injury well.

It hit me. He wasn't worried about me being gone for a few days. Something else was going on here.

"What's wrong?" I was hesitant to ask.

"I'm sorry." He placed a hand on my shoulder. "Your dad was captured on a mission. He's in Geuran."

At that moment everything in my world came to a crashing halt.

Acknowledgements

A huge thanks to my beta reader, my editor and my artist. Without their help I don't know where I would be.

I'm dedicating this book to my niece, Sarah.

To everyone who read this book, thank you. If you enjoyed it please take the time to leave a review.

For more information about the Outlander Leander series, visit http://o-leander.com/. "Beneath the Curtains: Outlander Leander Vol.2.5," a short story taking place between volume 2 and 3, is also available to read for free on the website.